T0158951

THE CAVE

FROM DARKNESS TO LIGHT

J. WILFRED, JR.

WESTBOW
P R E S S®
A DIVISION OF THOMAS NELSON
& ZONDERVAN

This is a work of fiction. All of the characters, names, incidents,
organizations, and dialogue in this novel are either the products
of the author's imagination or are used fictitiously.

Scripture quotations are taken from the Holy Bible, New Living
Translation, copyright ©1996, 2004, 2007, 2013, 2015 by Tyndale
House Foundation. Used by permission of Tyndale House Publishers,
Inc., Carol Stream, Illinois 60188. All rights reserved.

WestBow Press books may be ordered through booksellers or by contacting:

WestBow Press
A Division of Thomas Nelson & Zondervan
1663 Liberty Drive
Bloomington, IN 47403
www.westbowpress.com
1 (866) 928-1240

Because of the dynamic nature of the Internet, any web addresses or
links contained in this book may have changed since publication and
may no longer be valid. The views expressed in this work are solely those
of the author and do not necessarily reflect the views of the publisher,
and the publisher hereby disclaims any responsibility for them.

Any people depicted in stock imagery provided by Thinkstock are models,
and such images are being used for illustrative purposes only.
Certain stock imagery © Thinkstock.

ISBN: 978-1-5127-9624-7 (sc)
ISBN: 978-1-5127-9625-4 (hc)
ISBN: 978-1-5127-9623-0 (e)

Library of Congress Control Number: 2017911116

Print information available on the last page.

WestBow Press rev. date: 08/30/2018

CHAPTER ONE

Menacing darkness turned into blinding light. He ran as fast as he could away from the only home he'd ever known; his pale skin was slashed by shrubs and branches as he tumbled through this new, yet-unseen world. Falling almost as much as running, he felt dry leaves and grass sticking to cool sweat, mixed with warm blood all over his tired body. His young legs burned with exhaustion, but he had to get away—far away from the ominous cave.

A few minutes away, Aaron and Evelyn Freeman were fishing in their usual spot, not so much because they liked to fish but mostly to get away from their responsibilities at home. Aaron, the elder of the two siblings, was holding steadily to his fishing pole, hoping to add credibility to their excuse for being out all day. Evelyn, on the other hand, was carelessly splashing around the edge of the stream, helping their cause by looking for bait or anything moving, living, or slightly interesting. Aaron knew she didn't mind getting into trouble with their parents, because he always got the brunt of the punishment, since he was placed in charge of her. The only consolation he had was that she didn't get away with her childish antics and lame excuses as easily as she used to, since the birth of their baby sister Ilissa almost a year ago.

"Evelyn!" her brother scolded. "I told you to move away from here. You're scaring the fish away."

Evelyn continued splashing and responded with a smirk, "What fish? You've never caught a fish your whole life. Why do you think today's going to be different?"

Aaron was furious with her lack of cooperation, but why *should* today be different? She usually did as she pleased and got away with it. He decided to do the mature thing and just pick another spot, farther away from his immature little sister.

As he turned to walk away, he heard a huge splash, accompanied by his sister's piercing shriek. Aaron dropped his equipment, turned around, and sprinted toward Evelyn at full speed. His demeanor quickly changed when he saw the terror in his sister's face, as she pointed a few meters ahead of them and cried, "Monster!"

"That's no monster," he said as he ran past his sister and jumped into the water after the drowning boy.

Although the stream was fairly narrow, the current was strong enough to challenge any experienced swimmer … and he wasn't an experienced swimmer. His forward momentum was interrupted as soon as the water reached his waist, at which point he was forced to dive. The temperature and depth of the water tested his endurance; however, his biggest struggle came once he reached the young boy's arm. Out of breath and almost out of time, Aaron's lungs burned as he held the boy with one hand and reached for the surface with the other. A sudden burst of fresh air revived his senses, and he made his way to the shore to his little sister.

"He looks dead," she muttered as Aaron carried the boy to the shade of the trees.

Even though the small child was noticeably breathing, Aaron couldn't deny the fact of his sister's statement; the boy did, in fact, look dead. His skin was almost translucent and had no hue, except for bruises and recent scratches. He was extremely thin and dirty, in spite of his recent soaking in the stream.

"He smells dead too," Evelyn continued as she poked him with the fishing pole.

"Stop it!" Aaron scolded as he took off his shirt and used it to cover the boy's exposed body. "Let's take him home and get him cleaned up. Mom will know what to do."

They both lifted the frail, limp child and carried him home.

THEY ARRIVED TO A NOISY AND BUSY HOUSE. ILISSA WAS crying, and sounds of clattering pots and pans came from the kitchen. And even though it was past their lunchtime, exhaustion and the strange boy's smell had wiped out Aaron's hunger.

"Mom!" he yelled. "We need help."

"You need help?" their mother, Clara Freeman, replied from the next room. "I asked you two to help me hours ago. Where have you been? And what is that smell? It's like ..."

She stopped abruptly as she stormed into the living room and saw the unconscious boy on the floor. "Aaron, call your father," she ordered. "Evelyn, prepare a warm bath. Where did you find him? Is he okay?"

"He just fell into the stream," Evelyn said, "and we saved his life," she added as she rushed to fill the tub with warm water.

Clara quickly took Aaron's noxious, dingy shirt off the small boy and gave it to Evelyn to discard. She then carried the boy to the bathroom to wash him and disinfect his wounds. When Aaron came back without finding his father, she was already done cleaning the young boy, but he was still not conscious.

"Aaron," she said, "get me the smallest shirt you can find from your room."

He quickly obliged and helped dress the boy.

"It's way too big for him," Evelyn said.

"Well, what you do expect?" Aaron asked. "He's only about four years old."

"Settle down you two," their mother whispered as she carried him toward Evelyn's bedroom.

"Where are you going, Mom?" the girl asked. "Why don't you take him to Aaron's room?"

Clara quickly replied, "Your brother already gave up two shirts. We aren't going to make him give up his room as well. Besides, it's only a temporary arrangement."

She lay him gently on Evelyn's mattress as Aaron smiled at his sister, who stormed off.

There, the mysterious boy remained motionless and fell into a deep sleep.

CHAPTER TWO

The next day began for the Freeman family with some loud thumping sounds, before the morning star, Astra, had risen. The darkness and shadows added to the confusion of this early awakening, while the entire family (save Ilissa) converged upon the kitchen, which was the source of the tumult. William Freeman finally managed to light a candle as a small silhouette dashed under the table. Evelyn screamed with terror, which immediately caused the small, mysterious figure and Ilissa to start crying simultaneously. Clara grabbed Evelyn and quickly took her to the baby's room to calm them both down.

From a distance, Aaron and his father peered under the table, where they saw the young boy cowering in the shadows.

"It's okay," William reassured him, "I'm not going to hurt you." Instead of calming the fearful boy, it seemed the closer Father got to him, the more he covered his face and retreated toward the wall.

"Let me try, Dad," Aaron insisted. "Maybe he'll remember me."

Father deliberately backed away from the table and gave his son the candlestick.

The first thing Aaron noticed was that the boy's shirt sleeves were rolled up, and his hands and arms were covered with some sort of jelly. Somehow, he had also managed to get jelly on his knees and under his bare feet; maybe it was when he scampered under the table.

"Hello there, boy," Aaron whispered as he crawled under the table. "Remember me? I rescued you from drowning and carried you to my home. You're safe now."

His words and actions had the same effect as his father's, which confounded him greatly. Aaron decided to forcefully pull the boy out from under the table, so he put the candlestick down and reached for him with both hands. As he lay the candle aside, the boy uncovered his face and pointed nervously to the small flame.

"I don't think it's you he's afraid of," Father commented as he moved the candlestick above the table.

The boy then smiled at Aaron for the first time, as he came out from under the kitchen table.

Aaron noticed that the boy squinted at the dim candlelight, as if he was looking directly at the light from a thousand flames, and asked, "What's your name, little man?"

The young boy seemed to ignore the question and pointed Aaron to the spot near the pantry, where he planned to continue his early morning feast. There were bread crumbs and jelly marks, along with familiar and unfamiliar liquids, in the corner closest to the pantry. It soon became evident that the main ingredient of the pool on the floor was the young boy's urine.

"Did he have an accident?" Father asked while he grabbed vinegar, a mop, and a pail.

"I don't think so," replied Aaron. "His underwear's dry, and he smells like a clean jelly sandwich."

"He was probably marking his territory," Clara said casually as she walked into the kitchen. "There's another puddle next to his bed."

"My bed!" Evelyn declared firmly from another part of the house.

Clara took the boy into her arms, without any complaint on his part. She looked straight into his squinting eyes and lovingly asked, "What's your name, honey?"

Without warning, the young visitor grabbed Clara's ears with both hands, pulled her close, and licked her face from lips to forehead.

Aaron and Father both burst into laughter, which immediately attracted Evelyn into the room. "What's so funny?" she said in her most annoying, high-pitched voice. "The baby's still crying, my room smells like pee, there's a mess in here. And it's not even light out yet."

After a few seconds of complete stillness, the entire room exploded into laughter once again, which startled the boy in Clara's arms and caused Evelyn to storm out.

Aaron noticed the confusion in the mysterious boy's face and said, "I don't think he understands us. And why is he afraid of fire?"

Clara gave her husband a knowing glance but remained quiet.

"It's not the fire that bothers him. It's the light coming from the flame," William said as he examined the boy's physical features. "Where did you say you found him?"

━〕━

A GREAT DISTANCE AWAY, IN A PLACE OF PERPETUAL DARK-
ness, where neither the warmth nor the light of day
had ever been felt or seen, a lone, repulsive creature
marched toward his master. His muscular, olive-col-
ored body grew more tense with every step. Nabal, commander of the goblin army, was easily distinguished
from his troops due to the many tattoos on his body
and the scar over his left eye, which left him partially
blind. Sight was useless in this underground realm, but
even though his eyes could quickly adjust to light, his
handicap greatly hindered his abilities aboveground ...
and he and his master both knew it.

The time had come for his weekly report, and as
usual, he would get the blame for the news. He hated
his job, his limitations, his prison-like environment, but
most of all, he hated his master. It was his failed coup
that led them to this nightmarish abyss, where they
were more like guards than warriors. The only thing
that haunted Nabal more than their past failures was
their present wretched condition.

The increase of bioluminescent insects along the
walls, and the faint glowing orange outline of two
large doors, meant he had arrived at his destination.
He looked down at the smaller goblin guards as they
quickly opened the heavy metal doors for him to enter
the king's chamber. Apparently, it wasn't fast enough
for Nabal because he thrust both doors apart himself,
causing the guards to be thrown against the wall with
a great thud. His eyes quickly adjusted to the light from
the torches that surrounded the chamber, where the
infamous Goblin King sat slumped on his throne.

"What unpleasant news do you have to share with me today, Nabal?" the king inquired of his commander.

"Your royal highness ..." Nabal began but was quickly interrupted.

"Spare me your flatteries, fool," the king growled. "We both know that you aren't here because of your admiration of me. Just tell me what I need to know and skip the details so we can both continue with our other chores."

"Very well," Nabal calmly continued, "we lost another human ..."

"Of course you have, you imbecile," the king chimed in. "Have you found a way to seal the cave so we can stop them from escaping?"

Nabal, annoyed at the interruption, continued, with clenched hands and gritted teeth, "There's some sort of magic surrounding the opening that makes it impossible, Sire."

"Well, then, you're wasting my time," the exasperated Goblin King said. "Follow procedure and see if you can retrieve the beast. Next time we meet, I expect you to have better news for me."

CHAPTER THREE

D awn came quickly for the Freeman family, but as the morning got brighter, they all had to find creative ways to keep Evelyn's room as dim as possible for their new visitor. Before they closed the door and shutters completely, they decided that Aaron and Dad should stay in the room with the boy so Mom and Evelyn could take care of Ilissa and do the chores around the house that day.

The first challenge was finding a suitable name for the boy, since he seemed to only have a language of grunts and groans. "How about Gronk?" suggested Aaron whimsically.

"He's not our pet, Aaron," Father objected. "If my suspicions are correct, he will live with this new name for the rest of his life."

Aaron seemed confused and asked, "You mean he's staying with us forever? All right! I've always wanted a brother."

"Let's not get ahead of ourselves, son. I'll go talk to my friend Pat at the Justice Department after we break fast this morning."

They all stared at each other for a few moments, and then Father finally broke the silence: "He reminds me of a friend I had when I was young. He was smaller and thinner than all the boys his age, and he stuttered when he tried to speak. His name was Christopher Dale, and he lived at a home for orphans on the other side of town."

Aaron, anxious to get on with the more important details of the new family arrangement, pointed to the boy and enunciated, "Chris-tuh-fur," half expecting him to repeat after him. Frustrated after a few attempts, Aaron said, "Why don't we shorten it to Chris?"

He touched the boy's chest with his index finger as he repeated, "Chris." The boy's eyes widened, and a crooked smile revealed his yellow-tinted teeth as he repeated the sound and pointed to himself, saying, "Kwiss."

A loud pounding on the front door erased all their smiles. Swiftly, but without panicking, Father commanded Aaron to hide with Christopher in the bedroom closet.

"I don't understand," Aaron objected.

"I don't have time to explain. Just do it and stay hidden," Father said as he turned and walked away.

As William opened the bedroom door which led to their living room, the front door was kicked open by a large, olive-toned leg attached to the biggest goblin he had ever seen.

"What is the meaning of this?" Father demanded as he raced to protect his quivering wife and eldest daughter.

"We are here for the child," a short, intellectual-looking goblin named Maruffo said as he came through the door.

"No!" Clara screamed, flailing her arms as William restrained her.

"Many apologies for the door, Mr. and Mrs. Freeman. We have found in past operations that our property seems to vanish suspiciously if quick and drastic measures aren't taken."

"He is not your proper ..." Evelyn began, but Mother briskly covered her mouth.

"He?" Maruffo said quizzically. "My legal documents show that approximately eleven months ago, Ilissa Margaret Freeman was delivered in your household, and as you well know, the child becomes our property once it is weaned from its mother.

"Search the house!" he commanded his torch-wielding troops, as Father tried his best to hold his inconsolable wife.

Evelyn stepped in their path and screamed, "Take me instead!" while Ilissa began to whimper from her room.

The goblin enforcers didn't hesitate as they pushed Evelyn aside and went straight for the baby's room.

"Don't you dare touch my daughter!" William fumed as he watched Maruffo inch toward Evelyn with a sickly grin and a piece of dark fruit in hand. He knew the addictive passion fruit would be more than enough to seduce and enslave her indefinitely.

The goblin offered the sweet-smelling fruit to Evelyn, licked his sharp teeth, and said, "You are welcome to join us, child."

"Now you're crossing the line, fiend!" William yelled as he let go of his wife and pushed the goblin authority onto the floor.

He immediately felt a sharp pain as he struggled to move and breathe. The last thing he saw was the dull blade of a goblin sword protruding from his chest as he fell to the floor.

AARON WAS CLOSE ENOUGH TO HEAR EVERYTHING, BUT IT was his mother and sister's screams that finally convinced him to leave his hiding spot. He struggled to get up as Chris held tightly to both of his legs.

"Let me go," Aaron said in exasperation, tears burning his eyes. "Don't you understand? I need to help my family."

"IT IS A VIOLATION OF THE LAW TO ASSAULT AN OFFICIAL OF his majesty's army," Maruffo said plainly as he got up and straightened his neatly pressed uniform. "The punishment is immediate eviction. Torch this place," he snarled.

Evelyn felt Mother pulling her face away from the sight of her dying father. "Listen to me carefully," she said. "Go get the boys and climb out of your room through the window ..."

"What about you and Daddy?" Evelyn interrupted. The goblin soldiers were wasting no time setting everything in their sight on fire.

"I'll get Daddy out of the house; now you go. Hurry!" Maruffo and his gang of goblins walked indifferently out of the blaze, the last of which carried the crying baby girl under his muscular arm.

"What about Ilissa?" Evelyn asked in anguish.

"We can't save her," Clara said, conceding defeat, "but you need to help your brother now. Please ... run."

Her mother's words echoed in her ears as she stumbled to her room, grabbed a chair, and hurled it through her large window, pushing the shutters out with the force of the throw. Through the open closet doors, the boys stared dumbfounded at the shattered window and then at Evelyn.

Without hesitation, she removed the covers from her bed, placed them over the broken glass on the window sill, and screamed, "Go!"

THE BILLOWING CLOUD OF SMOKE SIGNALED THE NEARBY town of Woodland to come to the Freemans' aid. Sadly, the bucket brigade was too slow in putting out the fire, and the medics too late in saving William from his mortal wound.

Aaron ran to the nearest group of officials and said frantically, "Those animals who took my father's life also took my baby sister. If you hurry, you might be able to catch them."

Putting his arm around the boy, the chief officer took him aside and asked, "What's your name, young man?"

"We don't have time for this," Aaron said, brushing the official's arm away as he continued, "Are you going after them, or do I have to get justice myself?"

"Justice is different than revenge, son. We have to follow the law or risk starting a full-scale war against the entire goblin army," the officer replied.

"What kind of law allows those monsters to steal babies from their homes without consequence? I'm not starting a war; they're the ones who are bringing the war to us," Aaron screamed as he stomped away, disgusted.

As he walked toward the embers of their former home, his mother called out through sobs and tears, "Aaron, wait! What are you doing?"

Ignoring his mother, he found a shovel and began digging through the smoking remains.

Walking as close as she could without burning her bare feet, Clara cried, "I just lost two members of my family. I can't bear to lose a third."

The distress in his mother's voice pierced Aaron's soul. He dropped the spade, turned to look at his mother for the first time since hiding in Evelyn's room, and ran to her open arms as they knelt on the grass and wept.

CHAPTER FOUR

F amily was all the Freemans had left. Unbeknownst to the children, their rigid definition of family was about to be altered again. They traveled to their Aunt Sarah's country home, arriving late that afternoon; they all took turns bathing and filling their stomachs with warm vegetable soup. They hadn't seen their aunt or Cousin Freddy in many years, mainly due to their work that required them to travel regularly.

"How are the trade routes this year, Sarah?" Clara asked, forcing herself to sound interested.

"Oh honey, don't we have more important matters to discuss?" Sarah replied.

Clara insisted, "No, the children are present. Besides, it seems we only visit on holidays or in times of crisis, and I want to know how the rest of my family is doing."

Sarah hesitated slightly and then began, saying, "Well, we are making ends meet. Freddy is growing stronger each year and is able to help more and more with the heavy lifting. We also get harassed a lot less since most people think he's my husband, due to his size and facial hair."

Freddy flexed his biceps and puffed out his chest, saying, "I'll be seventeen this year. How old are you, Aaron?"

"Fifteen," he answered in a little more than a whisper.

"That's true," Freddy blurted. "Now I remember. You had trouble keeping up with me when they found us."

Everybody froze except Chris, who kept happily slurping on his soup.

"Found us? Who found us?" Aaron questioned and looked at his sister, who mirrored his look of confusion.

Freddy pressed his lips and excused himself from the room, hugging his mother on the way out.

"I gather you haven't told them," Sarah said frankly.

"Mom, what are they talking about?" Evelyn asked.

"I'm not your mother," she began. "Neither of yours … nor is Clara my birth name."

"That's not funny, Mom," Aaron snapped, as he stood in protest and continued, "Next thing you'll tell us is that Dad wasn't our father, and Sarah isn't your sister."

"I can't do this. Not now," Clara said, as she got up to leave the room.

Sarah stopped her at the door and told her, "It's time we told them the entire truth. I am with you." She then asked everybody to sit and called Freddy to take Chris outside with him.

She began, "My name *is* Sarah, and Clara *is* my sister, but these haven't always been our names, and this hasn't always been our life. As far as we know, we were both born in the cave many years ago. I don't remember too much about it, except some putrid smells that jog my memory back to those times in that smelly slave den.

"Clara was the first to discover the opening," she continued, "and she came back to tell a group of us about it. None of us were brave enough to go alone, but a young boy named Racá led us back to the opening, with Clara as our guide. We thought the goblin guards would be our greatest obstacle to escape, but instead it turned out to be the brilliant light coming from the outside of the cave; it stopped us many times. Racá noticed that there was a cycle of darkness and light outside the opening and timed our escape accordingly. One dark evening, seven of us said goodbye to our parents and left the cave, planning never to return."

"Seven?" Evelyn asked, as her eyes opened wide.

"Yes," Sarah continued. "We walked through the forest all night. It wasn't difficult to see through the darkness since, in our eyes at least, the stars were like fireworks illuminating this strange world. The trees reminded us of the stone pillars in the mines, but the soft grass was like nothing we'd ever seen. The sights and clean smells of this new environment suddenly awakened in us a desire to rid ourselves of our filthiness, so we bathed and played in a stream of clean, flowing water.

"Hungry and fatigued, we finally reached the edge of town escaping the blinding rays of the morning star. Forcing our eyes open, we were horrified to see a group of figures coming toward us. They placed thick sacks over our heads as they spoke to each other in an odd language. Our fear quickly evaporated as we realized that these gentle beings weren't taking us captive, but the exact opposite. They washed and clothed us as they slowly gained our trust and eventually nursed us to full health."

Aaron sat quietly while his sister eagerly asked, "Who were these people?"

Sarah paused and waited until both the siblings were looking at her; she answered, "They call themselves the Brotherhood, a group of former slaves who now oversee several branches of the Justice Department as well as the orphanage where we ended up. That loving group of dedicated men and women became our new family, who patiently taught us to read and write as well as the customs of our people. They even gave us new names; the youngest became known as Christopher, then we had shy little Maggie, the twins Jason and Jeremy, your mother, me, and the eldest of the group, William."

"Dad?" they both asked, with disbelief in their voices and tears in their eyes.

Clara spoke for the first time since her sister began recounting their story: "Your father and I grew to love each other deeply as the years rolled by. As young adults, we made a covenant to each other, and to our Lord Abba, to start a family and be faithful to each other, until …"

All the obstructed grief of the day suddenly burst out, as her body shook with every sob. The entire table joined in her sorrow as tears flowed freely for the next moments, which were too long and not long enough.

Freddie and their little visitor walked into the kitchen as the rest of family began to get up from the table, drying their tears as if they had just been released from a prison of lament.

"I just started a fire out ...," Freddie began saying, until he covered his own mouth and started whacking his own head.

In addition to the power to destroy, fire also has the power to purify, give warmth, and bring people together. It was apparent that the healing power of confession and forgiveness had cleansed the souls of the entire household, since they all, one by one, walked past Freddie and Chris, hugging them on their way outside to enjoy the cool night air.

BACK AT THE MOUTH OF THE CAVE, A SMALL ARMY OF GOB-lins, led by Nabal, were carrying out their urgent assignment. Explosions were detonated, and debris was carried to block to the opening, but their frustration grew as it became apparent that the task of sealing the slaves' escape route was impossible.

"Commander," one of guards said, "we haven't made any progress in closing off the cave entrance. The spell cast at the Emancipation hasn't worn off."

"Would you like to explain that to the king?" asked Nabal rhetorically. "Stop wasting time and keep working until Astra rises."

One of the younger guards asked timidly, "But if we seal the cave, how will we get out?"

The first guard stepped back as Nabal plodded toward them with a blank expression.

"The problem isn't us getting out," he replied. "We have no need of the outside world or these human slaves."

Nabal abruptly changed his demeanor and tone as he grabbed the young goblin by the throat and muttered, "We could easily get the young goblins to do all the work." The small goblin struggled to breathe as Nabal continued, "Your dependence on human labor has made you weak and stupid. You fail to see our advantage in strength, number, and experience." He squeezed the young guard's throat with a grimace. "I no longer have use for you," Nabal concluded, throwing the lifeless body across the field.

The remaining guard stood at attention, looking everywhere except the eyes of his commander.

"We are forgetting who we are," Nabal said, mostly to himself, "Our civilization has become nothing more than tricksters and babysitters, ignoring our history and having no vision for the future." Turning to the motionless goblin a few steps away, he growled, "Time is running out. Order half the troops to barricade the cave from the inside. If successful, we will once again use the King's Portal as we did before the wretched Emancipation."

CHRISTOPHER'S EYES DANCED WITH THE FLAMES OF THE campfire outside Sarah's cottage. He squinted less and less as the family passed the time, getting to know each other again.

The conversation abruptly turned serious as Aaron asked sheepishly, "So Mom, where did you find us?"

With just a moment's pause, Clara began, "Even though your father and I were legally ready to start a family, Abba had different plans for us. We were heart-broken as the years went by, and I was unable to have children of my own. In slight resignation, we decided that we should focus our time and energy helping the Brotherhood with the orphanage. It was no accident that they found us. As they raised us, they taught us the Histories, explaining how they were entrusted with the mission to seek and rescue any person coming out of the cave. Every evening, small groups of us would search the areas around town, being careful not to run into the goblin spies in the process."

"Late one night on one of those fateful excursions," she continued, "Sarah, your father, and I were out hunting for dinner. We had tracked a small boar to the rock bridge on the north side of town. It was Sarah who first crept under the bridge, drew her bow, and froze. When we caught up to her, she was still motionless, unsure if what she saw was animal or human. Goblins would many times use animals, or even their own young, to lure humans into traps. I stood between Sarah's bow and the creature, as your father vigilantly investigated her find. The smell was our first clue that this was no animal or goblin, and when three young babes began to cry, we were convinced it wasn't a trap."

"You found us under a bridge?" Evelyn asked, looking aghast.

"Isn't that amazing?" Freddy asked, stepping in. "I was probably only around five years old, and Aaron could barely walk. That's why you guys don't remember the cave."

Clara continued the story: "Many generations may pass without even seeing one person escape from the cave. We were overwhelmed, to say the least, at finding three, especially so young. Upon returning to the orphanage, William and I hastily requested to adopt all three of you. The Brotherhood suggested that we pray to Abba for guidance. For several nights, Freddie had recurring nightmares, leading him to wake up screaming; Sarah offered to raise him as her own, while Aaron and Eve came to live with us."

"I can't believe it," Aaron said, confused. "Why don't I remember any of this? Why didn't you tell us before?"

Clara moved to sit closer to both her adopted children; she put her arms around them and said plainly, "We were trying to protect you. The awful memories of the cave still haunt all of us."

They all turned to look at Christopher, who had fallen asleep on the ground. He was restless, and the expression of fear and pain on his face was the exact opposite as he had looked while he was awake.

"Come on, everybody," Sarah urged. "It's time for rest. I think we should visit the orphanage in the morning to see how we can help our little friend."

24

CHAPTER FIVE

Early the next morning, a knock at the door woke the entire Freeman family. Aunt Sarah opened the door and invited a plump, middle-aged woman in uniform into her home. Once again, Aaron stayed with Christopher in one of the bedrooms, while everyone else came out to meet the visitor, who had already taken off her hat as a sign of respect. The expression on her face gradually brought everyone's guard down as she introduced herself and expressed her condolences; she began, "My name is Patricia Towey, and I work for the Justice Department Research Division. The news about yesterday's incident has affected our entire community deeply. William was a respected public figure, as well as a personal friend of mine."

"So you're the Pat he spoke about," Clara said, finally making the connection. "I had imagined you … differently. William talked about how you had helped him petition the courts to pass stricter regulations on human/goblin interactions."

Ms. Towey sat down as Clara told Evelyn to fetch Aaron and Chris.

"Pat's a girl?" Aaron exclaimed as he walked into the room.

"Woman," Patricia corrected as she rose to meet the boys. "And who is this little guy?" she asked, looking at Christopher as he hid behind Aaron's leg.

Evelyn began rambling, "We rescued ... okay, Aaron rescued Christopher from drowning the day before yesterday, but we don't know where he came from or his real name, so we named him Christopher, or Chris for short."

She looked at Chris, who smiled crookedly as he came close to introduce himself by licking her outstretched hand and saying, "Kwiss."

The edges of Patricia's mouth rose slightly as she took a handkerchief out of her pocket to wipe the boy's saliva off her hand, saying, "Looks like you found yourselves an emancipated minor. First one to be seen in many years."

"What do you mean by emancipated?" Evelyn asked as she received, and reciprocated, a dopey look from her brother.

Patricia explained, "The Emancipation is a real historical event that occurred many generations ago. Before the opening to the cave even existed, mankind lived in the darkness as slaves to the Goblin King and his forces. His underground empire extended into the depths of our world but had no access to the surface that we know of. There aren't many documents in existence that recount what happened to our people during that time, but we do know that people had families and created their own distinct civilization, with very different customs."

Aaron added, "Like licking each other and peeing in public places."

Patricia chuckled and continued, "We can't learn much from this little guy, since he's so young, but he can learn a lot from us. They seem to develop language skills later in life than their surface-dwelling peers. Many things we've learned have come from older escaped slaves who have firsthand knowledge and experience of the underground territories. Once they learn our language, and we learn theirs, we add that information to the archives at the orphanage."

Sarah stood and invited everyone into the kitchen area to continue to conversation. They all sat to eat, and as soon as they had asked Abba to bless their meal, Evelyn inquired, "Mom, didn't you say you made an escape route from the cave?"

Clara smiled and corrected, "I didn't say I made a way, honey. I found the opening, and your father led us out, but it was there since way before I was born. The Brotherhood taught us that Abba didn't intend for us to live in darkness, so He became a human child through a human mother and lived with our people. He grew in size like we do, but He always knew who He was and why He had come."

"Some of our ancestors were intrigued by his teachings," she continued, "which were contradictory to the way they had lived for generations. He spoke about following a better way and being born from above. Many began to fear the attention He was getting from the goblin guards, who began to talk about killing Him and his followers."

"He knew his time was short, so He had his followers remove a wall of boulders that had blocked a previously unknown part of the cave. Leading the crowds quickly through the escape tunnel, He used his own hands to push through the final barrier to freedom."

"What I've never understood is how Abba could be in the heavens and underground at the same time," Evelyn protested.

Patricia asked Sarah for a writing stick and paper and with them wrote the words "I am here." "Whose words are on that paper, Evelyn?" she began.

"Yours," Evelyn quickly countered.

"Are there now two of me?" Patricia continued.

This time, Evelyn just stared at Patricia and waited for her to proceed.

"Abba's invisible, living Word was not written on paper but was instead surrounded by a human body that grew older, felt pain, and eventually died," Patricia said as she ripped the paper in half. "So now that my words on this paper are destroyed, does that mean that I am destroyed, as well?"

Clara smiled as she added, "That's why the Histories teach that our Creator humbled Himself, came down in the form of a slave, lived, and died among our ancestors: fully human and fully divine."

Evelyn objected, "But why did He have to die?"

Aunt Sarah replied quickly, "He didn't have to die. He chose to die. As He enlarged the opening to the cave, the people behind Him saw the rocks cutting into His strong hands. His wounds began to dissolve the final barrier between the cave dwellers and their freedom. They realized that this man was more than a prophet as they saw the supernatural power in His blood. The crowd began to exit the cave slowly but then began running as they realized they were being pursued. As our ancestors escaped, our Savior just stood there, blocking the way for the goblins, who pierced Him with their weapons. He called Himself 'Iam', but our people call Him the Emancipator because He willingly showed us the greatest love by laying down His life to set us free."

EXHAUSTED FROM WORKING ALL NIGHT, AND FRUSTRATED by his inability to please his king, Nabal took off his cumbersome, heavy armor and prepared himself for some rest. A rapid and consistent knock on his wooden door altered his plans, but not his mood. The fact that only officers would be allowed to contact Nabal in this manner did nothing to soften his response, as he angrily opened his door and yelled, "What is it?"

Maruffo let himself into Nabal's den and helped himself to a stool while saying, "Even though I do enjoy causing you inconvenience, this time I'm not here for my personal pleasure. I'm here by direct order from the King himself."

Nabal clenched his jaw as he countered, "Can't this wait?"

Maruffo smiled as he lit his pipe with one of Nabal's candles and replied, "I suppose it could, but it's so amusing to see the veins on your forehead and neck bulge when you're exasperated."

With a swift reverse roundhouse, Nabal kicked the stool out from under Maruffo, which caused him to fall flat on his back. He quickly rolled close, then over him while kneeling and brandishing a small blade.

With a crazed look in his eyes Nabal said, "Maybe it's time you amused me for a change."

Completely outraged, Maruffo yelped, "How dare you? You know I'm under the protection of the king. Get off me now, you savage."

Chuckling, Nabal pushed himself up, using Maruffo's face as leverage, and said, "Fine, let's get down to the purpose of your visit so you can get out of my sight and give me peace."

Maruffo helped himself up, dusted himself off, and began his report in a business-like tone. "Very well," he began, as he cleared his throat, "you should know that we had an incident in one of our operations yesterday. A well-known human named William Freeman was exterminated, and his house was burned to the ground."

Nabal was confused and pressed for details: "Your job is simple. Why didn't your men follow procedure?"

Maruffo interrupted, "The human became aggressive and assaulted me. One of my simpleminded guards impaled him from behind to protect me. What was I to do?"

"So you burned the entire house down?" Nabal asked, in irritation and disbelief. "Do you want to provoke them to war?"

Maruffo picked up his pipe from the floor and replied calmly, "That's exactly what I want to avoid. That's why I incinerated the evidence against us, and why I'm here giving you this report. Your job is simple, Nabal: Terminate the insurgence."

CHAPTER SIX

"A re you sure you're not going with us, Mom?" insisted Evelyn.

"I'm sorry, honey. Your Aunt Sarah and Freddie have to take a short business trip so they can be back in time for tomorrow's funeral, and I still have to make preparations. Pat will take good care of you and your brother today while you try to figure out how to help Chris, okay?"

Not wanting to separate from her mother so soon after the loss of her father, she continued nagging, "What about Ilissa? How are we going to get her back?"

She embraced her mother tightly as she began to weep, and her mother reciprocated as she murmured in her ear, "We'll figure it out, Eve. We've both lost so much, and it's going to hurt for a long time, but we still have each other and our heavenly Father. He'll walk with us through the pain and make the pieces fit at the end."

Somewhat satisfied with her mother's words of love and with a small kiss on the cheek, Evelyn finally let go.

The walk into and through town of Woodland took longer than expected, since many residents knew Patricia and recognized the Freeman children. A few people even asked about the youngest child, who was dressed in a cloak to protect his eyes and skin from the intense afternoon light. Unaware of the details of the previous day's intrusion, many assumed that Chris was actually young Ilissa and made comments like, "She's grown up so fast" and "Why is she covered like that in the middle of the day?" Pat was professional and proper in her interactions with the town people as they made their way to their destination.

THE ORPHANAGE WAS A VERY SECURE FACILITY, SUR-rounded by immense stone walls and guards protecting the gates.

As Patricia and her group approached the main gate, Aaron mused quietly, "This place is a fortress. Who are they trying to keep inside?"

Patricia overheard his comment and replied, "The walls aren't there to keep people in, but goblins out."

Next, she approached and greeted both guards with a hug; they opened the heavy iron doors to let them in. The children entered first, as Patricia exchanged pleasantries and made conversation with her friends at the gate. The front garden was empty, except for a distant figure who seemed to be tending the grounds and wore a robe like Christopher's. The thin man slowly rose, uncovered his head, and began to grunt loudly and incoherently. Aaron felt his heart drop as he saw Chris running away from them, rushing toward the man with clippers.

"No, Chris, wait!" they both screamed, but even if he had heard them, he wouldn't have understood what they were saying. The boy kept running.

The man's serious appearance remained unchanged until Christopher ran right passed him and through the unlocked front doors behind him.

"Ha! Gets them every time," said the man, whose face looked very different now that he was smiling.

"Jason, is that you?" Patricia asked as she hurried past the siblings and down the path to embrace the man. "It's hard to tell you guys apart from a distance. Where's Jeremy? How have you guys been? Goodness, where are my manners?" Pat turned to look at Aaron and Evelyn's bemused and frozen expressions. She began again, "Aaron and Evelyn Freeman, this is Jason Turner. He and his twin brother Jeremy are part of the Brotherhood; they run the orphanage."

Jason smiled at the children, extended his arm, and said, "It is a pleasure to meet you two. You can call me Groa-oo-mph."

Evelyn asked, "What did you say to Christopher?"

Jason paused for a second and then answered, "Oh, is that the emancipated boy's name? There's another Christopher here at the orphanage; he's in charge of the archives."

Aaron's eyes widened as he blurted, "You mean Christopher Dale's still here? And you and Jeremy are the twins! You knew my mom and dad, Clara and William Freeman."

Jason's smile disappeared as he asked, "*Knew* your parents?"

Patricia noticed her friend's concern and stepped in to clarify, saying, "Their home was attacked yesterday morning. The Goblin Guard came for their recently weaned baby sister, and they took William's life as well. We are here to place the emancipated minor under your care and to see how we can help the Freeman household."

Jason was speechless for an instant as tears welled up in his eyes. He then embraced both children and said, "I'm so sorry for your loss. Let's go inside and see what can be done."

The quietness from the garden dissolved as they walked into the entrance hall, where a crowd of children were sitting at tables and servers attempted to maintain order.

Jason began the informal tour by saying, "This is the reason you didn't see anybody outside playing or working. This room is used for eating, sleeping, and even recreation when the weather doesn't allow us to take the children outside. Chris should be in here somewhere."

"Brother Turner!" came the squeals from a group of children in the back of the room.

"I think we found him," said Patricia, as they all followed Jason to the commotion.

The serving line had come to a complete stop as the one of the children began to explain, "We were just coming to get a second serving when this boy cut in front of us and took most of the leftovers under the table with him."

Jason chuckled as he admitted, "That was probably my fault. I wasn't very specific when I invited him in."

Evelyn asked again, "So what did you say to Chris earlier?"

Jason went under the table to pull out the oblivious, disheveled boy as he explained, "All I said was, 'Food inside.'"

AFTER THEY ALL FILLED THEIR STOMACHS, BROTHER JASON continued the tour by taking them to the Admittance Department, where a group of volunteers, led by his twin brother, gladly began to process young Christopher.

"Not all our orphans come from the cave," he explained. "Many of the children who end up here are separated from their parents either by natural causes or by goblin attacks. The staff will be busy here with Chris for the next few hours, as they examine him medically and fill in the paperwork, but now it's time to deal with your situation," he said lovingly, as he directed them to the basement.

The children's first surprise was how bright and clean they kept the stairs and lower floor, but more surprising still were the amount of books and scrolls that filled the basement. Surrounded by stacks of books, a small thin man sat at a long wooden table, engrossed in his studies.

"Is that Christopher Dale?" Aaron whispered as they slowly walked toward him.

Jason just winked at them as he took a thick book from the shelves, opened it as he walked closer to the unsuspecting man, and slammed it closed right above his head. The sudden noise caused Brother Dale to yell in panic, and as he swiftly pushed away from the table, the back legs of his chair stuck to the floor. Columns of books tumbled like dominoes as he began the chain reaction by falling backwards.

"How may I help you, Brother Turner?" Brother Dale asked as he stood up, noticeably upset.

It took a while before the group could compose themselves and Jason could reply, through his laughter, "Many apologies, Brother. My intentions were not to cause you frustration nor additional work. We didn't see you upstairs during our midday meal, so I decided to bring our guests down to meet you."

Jason began the introductions, repeated his apologies, and quickly excused himself to return to his duties. Brother Dale appeared elated as Patricia shared the news of young Christopher's emancipation, but he was saddened by the tragedy that brought the Freeman children to the orphanage.

"The goblin authorities had no right to murder your father," Brother Dale began to say, visibly shaken. "I'm so sorry you had to go through that. He will be missed, but I promise, justice will be served."

"What about Ilissa?" Aaron asked, frowning.

Patricia once again stepped in before the miscommunication escalated into a heated debate; she said, "Children, your mother thought that maybe Brother Dale would be better equipped to explain the property law directly from the archives. That's why we brought you down here." Evelyn joined her brother by frowning and crossing her arms, as Patricia concluded, "I'm just the messenger. It wasn't my idea."

Brother Dale relented as he went back to retrieve a massive book, whose title was *The Histories: Volume 1*. He opened it carefully and began to instruct the children: "In the beginning, Abba created a heavenly host, a perfect race of angelic beings who saw His glory and lived to serve Him. Abba is love, and He wanted His creation to choose to love Him in return, so He gave them a free will, knowing that some would choose to love themselves more than their Creator."

Aaron sighed, rolled his eyes, and declared, "We are wasting time. If Abba's all-powerful, why didn't he just force them love Him more?"

"Love can't be taken," Brother Dale explained. "It has to be given freely. One angelic being, who was more beautiful and prideful than the rest, took it one step further. He not only rebelled, he also convinced one-third of his companions to help him overthrow Abba. Of course, the revolt failed, and he and his followers were cast out of the heavens to roam the physical world we know. Soundly defeated and feeling indignant, this fallen creature found our first ancestors, Ish and Ishah, who were made in Abba's own image."

"This seems familiar, but I have a question," Evelyn said, raising her hand. "Why did Abba send his enemy to the same place as our ancestors? Why didn't he protect them?"

Brother Dale smiled as he explained, "Once again, Abba gave our ancestors a free will and a choice, just as he had given the angelic beings. He also gave them instructions to follow that would protect them from his enemy's lies. Sadly, they chose to trust the enemy rather than their Creator, and from that point, they and their descendants became the Goblin King's property."

"What? That makes no sense," Aaron said. "The Goblin King tricked our ancestors, and we became his property?"

Patricia deflected Aaron's frustration toward herself as she politely asked to intervene. She began to give a true account from her childhood: "When I was a little girl, I found a rare striped wolf cub with its leg caught in a trap in the forest. It wasn't badly hurt, but it was very weak, as if it hadn't eaten for a long time. I fed it some fresh meat, gave it some water from my canister, and then set it free. Not surprisingly, this wolf cub followed me home, in spite of my many attempts to lose it. My parents questioned the wisdom in allowing me to have a wild animal as a pet but decided that eventually, its instinct would guide it back to the forest, where it belonged. I thought they were wrong but was glad they didn't make me get rid of it. I named her Sabre and spent much of the next few years caring for her, as our love for each other grew. Despite that, my parents were right about Sabre's instinct, which led her into the forest to hunt for days at a time. One day, she left, never to return."

Because of a long pause, it seemed like Patricia's story was over, but she eventually continued, "A few years after her disappearance, reports reached our family of a mountain hermit who would use striped wolves to hunt. I finally convinced my father to take me up the mountain to see if the man had seen Sabre during one of his hunts. To our astonishment, right in front of the hermit's cabin, tied to one of the cabin posts with a chain, I saw Sabre: malnourished and full of blisters. My cries for help were answered by the hermit himself, who came out from behind his home holding a bloody ax. His crooked teeth made his grin look villainous, as he approached us and asked what we were doing on his property.

My father explained that he seemed to have taken our pet and bravely asked that he set her free. The hermit introduced himself as Renald and proudly explained how he had lured Sabre to his cabin to mate with his ordinary wolves. My father offered to redeem Sabre and her pups for a month's wages, then two months, but the man just laughed in our faces and told us each animal was worth twice that amount. He then ordered us to leave and threatened to kill us if we came close to his property again."

"Did he mean you weren't supposed to come close to his cabin or to the wolves?" asked Evelyn.

"Both," Patricia said, clarifying, "You see, even though Sabre was tricked into slavery, she was not the only one to suffer. From that point on, all her offspring became property of that monster as well."

Aaron shook his head violently and said, "No. I can't accept that. Because of Ish's mistake, Ilissa is a now a slave to the Goblin King?"

He grabbed his sister's hand and turned to leave, but before they exited the basement, Brother Dale clarified in a loud voice, "Keep in mind, Ish's mistake has been corrected by the Emancipator."

"Aaron, let go of me," Evelyn protested. "I can't walk as fast as you."

He turned to her and cried, "You don't get it, do you? Neither Patricia nor the Brotherhood are going to help us rescue Ilissa. Dad's gone, so it's up to me to save her." He turned and walked directly into Brother Jason, who was coming back to check on them.

"You can't save her, Aaron," he said as he looked straight into Aaron's eyes. "There are many things that you still don't know about our enemy."

"Oh yeah, like what?" Aaron questioned as he pushed Brother Jason aside and walked away.

"How will you fight an immortal enemy?" Brother Jason verbally pushed back, which caused Aaron to stop.

"You're lying," he said without turning around; he closed his eyes and fists, preparing to fight his way out if he had to.

There were many things Aaron didn't know, the past few days had proven that, but he knew goblins were not immortal. Either his father had lied about killing a goblin scout out of self-defense many years ago, or Brother Jason was lying to him right now.

Aaron didn't feel secure anymore; not about his past, nor about his future, especially since in the present, he heard Brother Jason's heavy footsteps coming closer to him. What was the truth? Does the truth change as you grow older; as your perspectives change? Is it possible to trust the Histories as told from fallible and sometimes manipulating sources? Aaron felt Brother Jason's presence behind him, but he also felt another presence before him.

Abba, he prayed silently, *if You're real, I need You to guide me to the truth. Don't let me be deceived or deceive myself.*

Brother Jason softly placed his hand on Aaron's shoulder and said, "If you seek the truth, you will find it, and He will set you free. Iam's words are accurately written in *The Histories* by the Brotherhood, as guided by the Spirit of Abba. If you try to fight on your own, you will be deceived, just as Ish and his wife were deceived and taken captive. You must know the truth to fight the deception."

"What is the truth?" Aaron asked Brother Jason, turning and yielding his soul.

Brother Jason smiled and said, "Truth is a person, and that person is called Iam."

CHAPTER SEVEN

Evening came quickly as the entire orphanage prepared for their final meal of the day.

"It's getting late," remarked Evelyn. "Shouldn't we head home before dark? Mom's all alone and will be missing us."

Patricia looked past Evelyn as she answered with a smile, "She's not alone, and she won't miss you too much."

Evelyn's mouth usually worked faster than her brain, and this occasion was no different, as she whined, "I know Abba's with her, but Freddie and Aunt Sarah won't be back until tomorr … oh!" She turned and saw her mother, who was standing a few steps behind her, listening to the entire exchange. She ran over to embrace her.

Aaron quickly joined the family hug right before young Christopher jumped on all of them, turning the huddle into a dogpile.

"I'm glad to see you all too," Clara said through her laughter, trying to stop Chris from licking her face.

Patricia and Brother Jason helped them up as they greeted Clara in a more subdued fashion.

"It's good to see you after all these years," Jason said. "Please join us at the head table. We have much to discuss."

The group reminisced through dinner, as their conversation outlasted the light of day. First the residents made their way to bed, then the volunteers, and last of all, Patricia bid them a good night as she went home.

As usual, Chris fell asleep wherever he could find a clean spot on the floor, which happened to be under their table. The only ones left sitting in the large, empty room were Jason, his twin brother Jeremy, Clara, and her children.

"I haven't seen Maggie here," said Clara. "Have you heard from her lately?"

The twins just looked at each other hesitantly.

"Who's Maggie?" Evelyn asked as she yawned and rested her head on the table.

"Margaret was one of the seven who fled with us from the cave," explained Jeremy. "We haven't seen her for many years. Soon after Freddie, Aaron, and Evelyn were adopted, she became withdrawn."

Jason continued, "We thought she just missed spending time with Sarah, William, and you, but we found it was much more than that. She somehow became addicted to the goblin's passion fruit; we don't even know where she first tasted it. One morning, she just failed to show up for our first meal of the day, and when we investigated her dormitory, all we found were traces of the forbidden fruit."

"Tell me more about the passion fruit," begged Aaron.

Jason explained that there was more than one definition for the word "passion."

"We don't mean 'passion' in the sense of 'extreme love,' as in the case of Abba toward us. The passion fruit is actually better described as 'fruit of the suffering' or 'fruit causing suffering.' It's one of the goblin's most potent weapons against the entire human race."

Clara began to cry as she quietly quoted from their Scriptures, "Our enemy has come only to steal, kill, and destroy."

Jason finished the quote: "But the Emancipator came that we may have life, and have it to the full."

Evelyn fell asleep at the table as everyone started to rise. Jeremy whispered, "We have a private room prepared for you and your children to stay the night. We even added a bed for little Chris so he can see some familiar faces in case he wakes."

The twins carried the slumbering children up to a small room, while Aaron and his mother followed closely behind them. After dismissing themselves, the brothers retired to their own quarters, while Clara and her son ended the day in prayer.

DARKNESS SURROUNDED AARON, AS THE ONLY SOUNDS HE heard were his breath and his heartbeat, like a distant war drum. As the sounds intensified in his head, a far-off wail joined the chorus. The infant's cry seemed familiar, and it began to grow louder as he walked closer. His outstretched hands guided him along the stone corridor; the walls felt cold to the touch.

Ilissa! he thought to himself, as he began moving faster and the tunnel began to narrow.

Small blue specks on the walls and ceiling made it easier to see, but the fact that they were moving began to unnerve him. An indistinct orange glow at the end of the passage compelled him to run toward it as his baby sister's crying was gradually overpowered by a low, guttural chuckle.

"I'm coming!" he called out, but then he tripped on a rounded stalagmite and fell onto a carpet of crawling insects.

Unable to stand, his eyes quickly turned to the dreadful metal clang that both doors made as they swung open. The sudden, intense heat and light coming from the large cavern in front of him caused the insects that covered him to retreat into the darkness. He could clearly see his baby sister on her back on the floor, as a large dragon's claw slowly reached for her.

"She's mine," growled the monstrous voice as Aaron woke up in a panic.

His sudden and silent awakening aroused no one as he fell to his knees in the dark room. "Abba!" he cried. "Please protect Ilissa from the enemy. The darkness is overwhelming, and I'm so afraid. I miss her and my father so much. Please give me the strength and courage to rise against the forces of evil that surround us all."

The room began to brighten as Astra's rays began to pierce through the shadows. Calm began to replace the fear in Aaron's heart as the brilliant light entered his eyes.

As thoughts of peace filled his mind, he felt as if Abba answered his prayer by whispering, "Light has come to overcome the darkness, and the gates of the underworld will not prevail against it. Victory over deception is found in the truth, and the truth you seek is found in Me."

Aaron rose to his feet, unsure of what the future held for his family but confident that his Creator had not forsaken them.

WILLIAM FREEMAN'S FUNERAL THAT AFTERNOON WAS ATtended by hundreds of people from Woodland and its surrounding communities. As they walked to their seats, Evelyn was the first to notice Patricia, her cousin Freddie, and Aunt Sarah in the multitude, but she also noticed something else.

"Aaron," she murmured, "why are so many people wearing armor and carrying weapons?"

It took awhile for her brother to respond, so she shook him and asked again.

"I don't know," he finally snapped, clearly upset that his sister wasn't paying attention to their mother's eulogy. "Maybe they're afraid the goblins will interfere with the service."

Her brother's thoughtless answer didn't satisfy her curiosity as she continued to scan the crowd for other clues.

As Brother Jason began speaking, it became clear that many attendees weren't there to mourn, as a wave of restlessness rippled towards the front.

One man waved his sword and shouted angrily, "I'm sorry, but we are tired of doing nothing while our people are terrorized and struck down. How are we supposed to turn the other cheek and ignore these constant attacks?"

Brother Jason tried to calm the mob by responding, "It is not our place to return evil for evil. Abba will bring the lawbreakers to justice in His time."

"We are tired of waiting for Abba's justice," interjected a woman from another part of the crowd as they began to leave.

The Brotherhood stood in unison, trying to restrain the disorder, to no avail.

"Where are they going?" Evelyn asked, in a panic.

"To the cave," Aaron replied, "and I'm going with them."

Brother Jason noticed Clara and Evelyn pleading with Aaron, so he left the podium and ran to them to assist.

He got in front of the young man and placed both hands on his shoulders, saying, "Aaron, you've got to listen to me. This is a mistake."

Aaron quickly brushed Brother Jason's arms away, snapping, "No. You told me the goblins are immortal, but my father told me he killed one when he was younger. Are you calling my father a liar?"

Evelyn thought Brother Jason was about to cry as he explained, "The truth is, I was there when William killed that goblin scout, but it wasn't a goblin. It was a goblin spawn called a Nephilim."

Then their mother came over and embraced Aaron. "It's true," she said. "I was there also."

Brother Jason then added, "Let me teach you more about the Histories and Abba's plan to bring our enemies to justice."

The Freeman family followed Brother Jason back to the orphanage as a great multitude went the opposite way, towards the cave.

CHAPTER EIGHT

B rother Jason and Brother Dale took the entire afternoon and evening, teaching the Freeman children facts about the Histories that the angry mob had overlooked. They reviewed with them how the disobedient spirits that were cast out of the heavens wanted dominion over humans, who were made in Abba's image. They talked in detail about how Ish, the first man, was deceived into selling himself and his descendants into slavery by ignoring Abba's commands.

After a few hours, Jason began to reveal some mysteries about their enemy and his offspring. He explained, "All created spirits are immortal. They have a beginning, but they will have no end. The Goblin King is actually a spirit who has taken possession of many human bodies over time. As the host grows old and eventually dies, the Goblin King's spirit just looks for another body to control. Any goblin that you try to kill will either heal itself or just roam around the underground in spirit form until it finds another body to possess. They have also been known to reproduce by taking human form and making human women their wives. Their offspring are the abominations known as Nephilim: half-human and half-goblin."

"So the Nephilim are mortal?" asked Aaron.

"Yes," Jason answered cautiously, "but even if we destroyed them all, the goblins could just produce more offspring. Plus, you would have to go through hundreds of immortal goblins to find and kill a single Nephilim." He paused and asked, "Do you understand the danger?"

Aaron nodded slightly and then stood suddenly and said, "We have to stop the townspeople from reaching the cave."

Frustrated by their powerlessness, Brother Dale sighed, "Sadly, they wouldn't listen to us. All we can do is protect the ones who stayed in town from the goblin retaliation."

THE CAVE RUMBLED WITH ACTIVITY AS THE CORRIDORS were filled with confusion. Fear added to the bewilderment of the infants, who were too young to understand their surroundings. Jumbled among the filth and mass of native young ones, Ilissa sat on the dark and dingy cavern floor. Inconsolable and starving since her abduction, she was unable to comprehend the disappearance of her sight and her enhanced sense of smell. Nothing in her new environment was familiar or even slightly pleasant. The stench of rotting food was covered up by the smell of feces and urine all around her. Insects crawled all over her as human hands of all sizes pushed, pulled, and yanked at every part of her bruised body.

Her new environment was normal to the native cave children, who competed with each other for their caretakers' attention. The blend of mothers and maiden volunteers, whose job it was to care for the community's infants and children, did their best to raise and care for each one in their usual troglodyte way, even the strange visitors the goblins brought to them. Daily they would attempt to feed them scraps, play with them, and teach them their unique language and customs as their parents worked in the mines. But today was different.

THE GOBLINS WERE PREPARING FOR WAR AND INCREASING their human labor force to produce weapons, armor, and other supplies. The fact that their parents were overdue to take them home had not been overlooked by the children, who knew their routine. Desperate to calm the children, one of the young ladies grunted a message to her superiors and ran home against the current of marching soldiers. Pushing her way back through the waves of goblin warriors, she finally returned to her designated area, carrying a huge covered basket. Some women immediately recognized the faint smell that returned with the maiden and argued against her suggestion. Others insisted that this was the only way to pacify the confused and hungry children, since their daily rations were spent. One by one, the women either agreed or left as the dark fruit was distributed to every child.

FOR THE FIRST TIME SINCE HER ARRIVAL, ILISSA RECEIVED something desirable in her hands, and as she took a bite of the soft and sweet-smelling fruit, her pain began to disappear, along with her hunger. First, her physical pain began to fade, as a strange arousal took its place. Next, the memories of her family were slowly forgotten as she stared at the unusual glowing lights that seemed to dance on the cave ceiling. Faces and voices in her mind mutated, as the line between reality and fantasy blurred and then seemed to dissolve.

The passage of time was ignored by Ilissa, whose body craved nothing but the passion fruit that was constantly being given to her to keep her quiet. She didn't notice the other children who had stopped receiving the addictive fruit, nor the fact that more and more of them were not going home to their parents, who were literally being worked to death. Her new home became the only home she remembered, as the unclean became clean and the bad became good in her mind. She was now a willing slave to the passion fruit and to her goblin masters.

BATTLE AFTER BATTLE, THE CHILDREN'S CHAMBER BECAME overcrowded with native and surface-dweller orphans as the women caretakers discussed their situation. Ilissa was about three years old now, but her addiction to the passion fruit kept her from communicating, understanding, or learning in any language.

The elders decided to separate children in smaller groups by size and gender in order to look after their growing needs. Many were taken in small groups to other parts of the cave, while a small portion were distributed into widows' homes.

Ilissa felt herself being lifted off the floor and pushed into the arms of an unknown woman. She barely noticed the other three girls her size following them, as the elderly woman did her best to guard against her constant attacks as she was dragged down an unfamiliar path. As the effects of the forbidden fruit wore off, Ilissa grew more violent as she struggled to free herself. She was distracted by interesting new smells throughout their walk, but one smell finally changed her anger and confusion to excitement. As the widow let go of Ilissa's arm, the smell of fresh passion fruit led her straight to her new home.

THEY CALLED THE ELDERLY WOMAN RUOK. SHE WAS HOSPItable and did the best she could to provide for the orphan girls. She made no distinction between the two who came from the surface and the two she knew from birth. In spite of the war raging aboveground, her home became a sanctuary to the girls, where they began to learn the troglodyte ways and customs.

The woman knew Ilissa's mental and physical growth would be greatly affected by her addiction to the passion fruit because of her age, so she began to limit her consumption of it. She wouldn't eliminate the use of the fruit completely, since it was one of her people's most abundant sources of food, but she would instead use it as a tool to manage and teach the girls. Whenever they followed her instructions, she would give them a taste of passion fruit juice, diluted with water. In Ilissa's case, she used the juice to calm her down and get her ready to sleep.

To keep the peace, the troglodyte widow designated an area for each of the girls, showing them how to mark it themselves and how to defend it from intruders and each other. She taught them basic commands and phrases by grunting, groaning, and screaming if necessary. She rewarded their progress by licking their faces and giving them treats like glowworms and slices of the coveted passion fruit.

She showed them how to calculate the passage of time by measuring the stalactites formed by water dripping on her corner of the den. They quickly learned how to quench their thirst by drinking the pools that collected from the runoff and how to satisfy their hunger by eating the insects that crawled around them.

As the stalactites merged with the stalagmites, they explored more of their dark world, from the great river to the expansive passion fruit fields. They became skilled at evading the goblin guards, who were more interested in winning their war and expanding their kingdom. As the four girls approached adolescence, they learned about their underground culture, but not about their history. The widow never told them about their true origins or who the goblins were fighting, but she knew they didn't really care. All that mattered to them was that they were content and that the cave would never stop producing their precious passion fruit.

CHAPTER NINE

Evelyn knelt beside her parents' graves as Aaron stood behind her. The ten-year Goblin War was over, and the losses to the Freeman family and the town of Woodland were immense. It seemed like the only things that remained standing were Aaron and the orphanage where the Brotherhood took refuge. Most townspeople has either moved far from the cave or died trying to fight the immortal goblins and their Nephilim offspring. Evelyn, now a young woman, could shed no more tears as she thought of how much their lives had changed since they had found Christopher.

"Our childhood seems like a distant dream," she mused, mainly to herself. "Our innocence and our family have been stolen from us by those wretched goblins."

"The war is over, Evelyn. Mom, Dad, Freddie, and Aunt Clara are now in their eternal home with Abba," Aaron said. "We need to seek His guidance as we rebuild our lives and the town."

Evelyn quickly stood and faced her brother as she lost control of her emotions; she cried, "Rebuild? How do you plan to do that, Aaron? There is no reason for us to stay. There's nothing here but dust, ashes, and painful memories."

"What about Ilissa?" Aaron countered quickly.

Evelyn sighed heavily and ran her fingers though her long, dark hair as she looked at the sky in desperation. She knew Aaron was right. The hope of finding and rescuing their sister was the only reason they had stayed at the orphanage all this time.

"We don't even know if she's alive," she said dejectedly. "It's been ten years."

Aaron walked toward his sister and gave her a strong but loving embrace as he whispered, "As long as there is breath in my lungs, strength in my body, and a glimmer of hope, I will try to save my sister. I would do the same for you." He put one arm around her shoulder as they began to head back to the orphanage and concluded by saying, "Besides, you know Ilissa isn't the only slave who needs to be saved."

FOR THE MOST PART, THE TROGLODYTE POPULATION WAS unaware that there had been a conflict between the goblins and the surface dwellers. They continued eating and drinking, living and dying, as they only paid attention to whatever brought them temporal happiness in their daily, meaningless existence. They created and worshiped gods made in their own image by fabricating festivals to mark the passing days. The greatest of their celebrations was dedicated to their god of the underworld: Hades.

Unbeknownst to the cave dwellers, their images of Hades were exact representations of the many forms the Goblin King had taken over the years. He had the power to influence his slaves by hijacking their thoughts and even reveal himself through dreams. What the troglodytes celebrated as simple revelry and fantasy was actually based on, and indirectly honored, their dark master.

Ilissa and her stepsisters were excitedly preparing for the festivity known to them as "Doo-rah," where a young maiden of eligible age would be chosen and dedicated to Hades. They had no idea that the chosen girl would be enslaved in the Goblin King's personal chamber, nor did they understand the suffering she would endure until a replacement was chosen and she was then sacrificed. All the girls were told was that one of the hundreds of maidens would be picked and taken to a place of honor, where she could get as much passion fruit as she wanted and would have no desire to return home.

Ilissa's mind wandered as she licked her hair in an attempt to groom herself. She thought back to one of the first young women she could remember being selected as Hades's offering. For some strange reason, that girl resisted and screamed as the elders forcefully took her into the depths of the cave. Ilissa understood the apprehension of not being able to stay with her people, but wasn't the promise of a life of pleasure worth the loss of friends and family?

Without warning, a vision of a strange place interrupted her thoughts. She was surrounded by light and felt a peace she had never felt before. The ground was clean and made of strips of brown organic material. Large rectangular openings on the painted walls sucked in long beams of light and then projected their shapes onto the floor. Her eyes opened wide to the bright, unfamiliar beauty around her. The joy and peace she felt were suddenly stolen by a large shadow that gradually blocked the light coming from the opening before her. The silhouette of a goblin guard grew larger as he came into the room and stretched his arms to grab her.

She startled herself as if waking from a dream, and her subsequent screech caused her stepsisters to retreat, while her adopted mother ran toward her. Taking Ilissa in her arms, she hummed a familiar tune until they both stopped shaking. She always saw herself as different from all of her adopted sisters, even the one named Tupi, who also came from the surface. Since their memories of the outside world had all but disappeared, the surface of their planet and its inhabitants remained one of the greatest mysteries to them.

Young Christopher had not only appropriated Brother Dale's first name, he also took on his responsibilities in the orphanage after the latter died in the goblin wars. Now approximately the same age Aaron Freeman was when he rescued him, Chris diligently studied the Histories as a passion inside him grew. He knew for a fact that he was a son of Abba and that the Emancipator had given his life to set him free. He also recognized the Spirit of Abba urging him to learn as much as he could so that he could lead his people out of the cave. But his calling had turned into an obsession that had caused him to neglect his friends and his health.

Coming down to the library, Brother Jason was amazed at how much young Christopher resembled his namesake as he poured himself into his studies. As Jason approached the studious teenager, he took a large book from the shelves and thought about how he missed Brother Christopher almost as much as his own twin brother. They all knew the risk they were taking by infiltrating the underworld to find and destroy the Goblin King's portal to end the war.

"May I be of assistance, Brother Jason?" Christopher asked, startling him out of his daze.

It took a split-second for Jason to recall the matter that had brought him to the basement in the first place. He began, "Your friends have been inquiring about you. It seems you've missed several meals and planned activities." He looked behind Christopher to see diagrams and manuscripts as well as a blanket on the floor. "Have you been sleeping down here?"

Christopher was noticeably embarrassed as he rose to tidy his desk and makeshift dormitory.

Jason placed his hands on the young man's shoulders to stop him long enough to say, "I know you want to go into the cave to find your family and free the slaves, but to do that, you need to feed your body and spirit as much as you're feeding your mind. Your knowledge of their language and wisdom from the Histories isn't going to save them. Only the Spirit of Abba can do that."

Unexpectedly, Christopher collapsed into his open arms just as Aaron and Evelyn walked into the library.

"Is he okay?" they exclaimed in unison as they ran to help Jason carry the weight of Chris's limp body.

"He hasn't been eating and might be dehydrated as well. Help me get him upstairs," Brother Jason said in a quick but calm tone.

Aaron lifted Christopher's torso from his arms as Evelyn and James each held a leg as they went upstairs.

They spent the entire day nursing Christopher back to health as Aaron, Evelyn, and Brother Jason kept him company. They shared how they felt the first time they took care of Chris after he almost drowned in the stream. They mourned the loss of William and how Chris never really had an opportunity to get to know him. Brother Jason, who had become a father figure to all three, took the opportunity to remind them that "all things work together for good" in Abba's sovereign plan, and that all his children would be reunited in eternity. Then the room became silent as they each processed what that meant for each of them and for the people who were held captive in the cave.

The quiet interlude was broken by Brother Jason as he divulged, "I think the time has come to infiltrate the enemy's camp. Get some rest, all of you. Tomorrow morning, after we break fast and pray, we have some training to do."

AS THE ORPHANAGE SETTLED FOR THE NIGHT, THE UNDERground dwellers worked themselves into a frenzy as the climax of Doo-rah drew near. The crowd chanted in a passion fruit-induced high as they linked hands and danced around the eligible maidens. The young girls gyrated wildly, trying to impress the dark priest as he examined each of them closely. Still shaken from her vision that afternoon, Ilissa did her best to mimic the movements of her sisters to blend in with rest of the group. Even though her flesh craved the fruit, she had decided not to consume any so she could be so-ber-minded throughout the selection process. She wanted to remember this night and try to understand the fear in the girl chosen so many years ago; that fear was now consuming her.

The chanting and drumming reached a fever pitch; some girls passed out from exhaustion, and others vom-ited uncontrollably, causing the crowd to widen the cir-cle. The offensive smell once again reminded Ilissa of the night the girl was taken against her will; she fell to her knees and began to tremble, trying her best not to lose her lunch. Behind her twirled her stepsister Tupi, who was lost in a trance.

Like a predator closing in on its prey, the priest walked barefoot over the unclean cave floor toward Ilissa and Tupi. Looking up just as the dark priest ap-proached, Ilissa shrieked in fear, thinking she had been chosen. In one quick motion, the priest slapped her and reached over to grab Tupi by her curly hair. The crowd roared as he lifted his scepter with one hand and held her erect like a trophy with the other hand. Ilissa tried to stand to obstruct the celebration, but the slimy floor caused her to slip and smash her head on the hard floor. The last thing she saw before she passed out was Tupi's eyes widen as she was swallowed by the multitude.

CHAPTER TEN

Aaron woke to a feeling of desperation as he knelt to pray, "Abba, I feel powerless to save my sister, much less the whole cave-dwelling population. I know that Ish unknowingly sold himself and all his descendants into slavery, but I also know that you sent the Emancipator to open the way to freedom. Please guide us so we may guide others to freedom. In Iam's name …"

"Amen!" Chris and Evelyn said as they smiled over Aaron. "C'mon, we're already late," Chris said, as he was the first out the door.

Aaron could feel his heart racing as he anticipated seeing Brother Jason at the mess hall, but he grew unsettled when they couldn't find him. They quickly ate their first meal and cleaned up, as there was still no sign of Jason anywhere. The last place they thought to look was Jason's own bedroom; they found him lying facedown, flat on the floor.

Aaron ran to him and said, "Brother," but his concern for him quickly faded as Jason got up, dusted himself off, and said, "What took you so long? Follow me."

Aaron expected Brother Jason to lead them outside to train, so he was visibly baffled when he began to lead them up the stairs instead of down.

"Where are we going?" asked Evelyn, who still had trouble keeping her thoughts to herself.

Jason either didn't hear or simply ignored the question as he labored through every step and breath.

The locked attic door opened slowly as Jason turned the key. They all followed him through the door into a hall they already knew was there. It was a narrow space, but big enough for all four of them to stand without bumping into each other. The trio just stood quietly between two hall doors, as Jason locked the first door from inside. Aaron's bewilderment grew as he walked past them to a painting hanging at the end of the hall. Brother Jason seemed to be enjoying keeping them in suspense as he looked back and smiled at them. He then removed the picture from its frame, exposing a strange metal mechanism embedded in the brick wall. After he carefully placed the painting on the ground, he began to turn each gear until a "click" verified the correct combination.

"Now we push," he said to the group as they joined in turning the stone wall 90 degrees to expose a secret room.

The thin layer of dust exposed evidence of previous activity instead of hiding it. Footprints on the floor as well as handprints on the large wooden chest made it obvious that they weren't the first ones to be showed the room.

"Why are we here, Brother Jason?" Christopher asked. "Didn't you say we were going to train today? We're losing valuable daytime."

Brother Jason knelt before the wooden chest to unlock it as he said, "The enemy's weapons are spiritual in nature; therefore, we need to train spiritually. We aren't going to start another war with the goblins. We are going to set the captives free." Jason pulled out a golden robe.

"Are we going to give them clothes to free them from fashion prison?" Evelyn joked.

"Don't be silly," said Jason as he gave a robe to each of them. "These are for you."

Ilissa woke in darkness to the sound of her name. It wasn't the name given to her by her stepmother, nor a name she remembered in her mind or heard with her ears. It was more like a kiss to her soul, as she felt the repeating whisper: "Ilissa … Ilissa."

She walked around the sleeping masses, careful not to step on anyone as she held her breath. For the first time she could remember, she could distinguish the offensive smells of liquids and gases emanating from the unconscious humanity in the cave. Her eyes burned and her lungs ached as she stopped herself from inhaling for as long as possible. The relief that came every time she exhaled was enhanced by the exhilaration of the sound of her name: "Ilissaaaaah."

She wasn't sure if she was just hearing her own breath until she got far away from the troglodyte camp, farther from the noises of the goblin guards. "Ilissa" she clearly heard as she followed the underground river until her legs grew weary. She stopped to refresh herself in the still waters and then froze when she saw her dim reflection. Her dark eyes and pale, thin features slowly metamorphosed into a beautiful and clean young woman. She stared in wonder for a few seconds as she ran her fingers through her hair and stroked her cheek.

When her actual reflection returned, she jumped back in horror and threw a rock into the water. Desperate to see the beautiful image of herself again, she dove in the cold water and did her best to wash herself and her clothes, with poor results.

Her frustration as she scrubbed kept her from hearing her name again until she finally gave up trying to clean herself. "Ilissa," came a whisper from the tunnel, farther ahead. Wet and still dirty, her clothes stuck to her body like a second layer of skin and slowed her progress down the cold tunnel.

The whisper grew louder as she came to a place she hadn't known before. She felt noticeably warmer as she looked downward to see a wall of rubble guarded by two large goblins. She crept as close to the ledge as she could without being seen; she could feel the warmth coming from the stones, but she could also see small rays of light that pierced through and hurt her eyes. From that point on, she knew that her destiny lay beyond the wall of rubble.

"I'VE HEARD OF LIGHT ARMOR BEFORE, BUT THIS WASN'T what I expected," said Aaron as he tried on his robe.

"It's not light armor; it's called the 'armor of light,'" Brother Jason corrected as he helped Christopher with his oversized garment.

"How is this supposed to help us save the prisoners?" Evelyn asked as she pulled the hood over her head and face.

"This special material was given to us by Abba Himself," explained Jason. "It refracts light in a way that makes you invisible to the goblins, but to the troglodytes, you will appear to shine. Eventually, their eyes will become accustomed to the faint glow, and you will be able to communicate with them. However, the goblins will always be able to smell you, even if they can't see you."

"Why didn't the Brotherhood use this advantage during the goblin wars?" she pressed. "So many lives could have been spared."

Brother Jason felt the emotion in Evelyn's voice, which triggered a temporary loss in composure. The loss of his friends and family in the battles and covert missions over the last ten years still made his soul ache with sadness.

He wiped his tired, tear-filled eyes and said, "The reason we didn't lose it all was because my brother led a small band of brave volunteers into the cave. They destroyed the king's portal and ended the war using the stealth provided by the armor of light. Only these three robes remain."

After a moment of silence, they exited the room behind Brother Jason, who made sure to conceal the secret entrance. He walked halfway down the hall, where two wooden doors faced each other. Unlocking one of the doors, Jason invited the trio inside the bright, empty room. The large stained-glass window drew in warmth and sent multicolored rays of light to every corner as they knelt on the floor.

Jason smiled as he began to teach, "The armor you're wearing has no power on its own. Its radiance comes from the Spirit of Abba, Who abides only in His children. Fear and lack of faith will expose you to the enemy, so it is important that you remember that His Spirit lives in you and will protect you in the darkest of places. Do your best to keep it clean, and whatever you do, don't take it off in the cave. At first, your radiance and smell will be offensive to the troglodytes, but the deeper you go into the cave and the longer you spend underground, the more they will tolerate you because you will begin to look and smell like them. Also, the longer you are away from the surface, the more you will start to think and act like them, so be careful. Let's ask for Abba's Spirit to guide us."

After kneeling to pray for a long while, Brother Jason rose and anointed each of them with oil, saying, "This oil is a symbol of the Spirit of Abba that is in you. I bless you in the name of Abba, His Son, and His Spirit."

When they opened their eyes, their robes seemed more radiant. They couldn't tell if they were truly brighter or if it was just an illusion, due to the fact that they had their eyes closed for so long, but whatever the case, they felt ready to face anything.

Brother Jason couldn't hide his childlike glee as he quickly motioned for the group to follow him. When they locked the door behind them, they all correctly guessed where they would go next. They went through the other door into a dark, equally empty room with no windows. Once that room's door was locked behind them, the only light they could see was the glow of their robes and a small strip from the bottom of the door that seemed to direct them to a stone fireplace at the far side of the room.

They slowly followed Jason as he cautiously went into the opening and down a metal ladder that was welded to the chimney's inner wall.

"So this is why we never use the fireplace in the mess hall," said Christopher, who was quickly shushed by the group.

They descended past a wall that separated the main fireplace from the false chimney and continued downward.

"Are we going to the basement library?" whispered Chris.

"We are going to the armory *under* the library," emphasized Brother Jason as Evelyn gasped.

She was the last of them to reach the floor of the armory, where they discovered supplies and weapons of every kind. Brother Jason finished lighting the torches and waited patiently for the three of them to examine the human and goblin artifacts in the collection as he sat on a barrel in the middle of the room. Aaron gravitated toward the different types of metal armor displayed along the walls, while his sister followed Chris to the unusual weapons.

"Can you teach us to use all this?" Aaron asked excitedly.

"Actually, all you'll need for your first mission is this," Jason responded, as he pointed to the barrels.

"What is that?" Evelyn asked, confounded.

Brother Jason stood as he used his body language to emphasize his response, "Explosives."

CHAPER ELEVEN

Ilissa's excitement was obvious to her stepfamily as she returned to the den for supplies. Her stepmother backed away in fear as Ilissa described her journey to the secret passage to the goblin barricade. The old woman had heard distressing tales of troglodytes who had gone missing after following that path and begged Ilissa not to go there again. Ilissa tried to comfort her by explaining the peace she felt as she followed a whisper through the warm tunnel with the strange, radiant rocks. Her older stepsister, Uka, was intrigued by the story and volunteered to accompany Ilissa while their youngest sister, Aur, stayed with Ruok. After accumulating provisions and binding their sleeping mats, they said their goodbyes and began their excursion through this previously unknown part of the cave.

The journey was longer than Ilissa remembered. They passed the mines where most of the adults would labor to find metals to melt and shape into their tools. They stopped to rest at the fields where their people would grow mushrooms and the infamous passion fruit. Uka helped herself to a fruit and offered her stepsister a portion. Even though their bodies had become somewhat resistant to the effects of the fruit and it would take several to intoxicate them, Ilissa declined and picked some mushrooms instead. She wondered to herself if her cravings had diminished naturally or because of her excitement to see beyond the glowing barricade.

Once they had their fill and massaged each other's bare feet, they continued their trek through the darkness, following the underground river. Ilissa hurried as she remembered the place where she had bathed and gone through a cold, cloaked passage on the other side of the river. She could tell Uka was reluctant to get wet since, traditionally, water was for drinking and not for swimming. For the first time since they began their expedition, her sister's enthusiasm began to visibly fade as she waded through the water.

She noticed Uka's frustration growing as the promise of warmth remained unfulfilled on the other side of the underground river. Ilissa urged her through the passage which led to the magical place and found nothing but a pile of cold rocks, next to two sleeping goblin guards. Visibly confused, Ilissa tried to explain how everything was different now, but Uka wouldn't listen. On the ledge and still hidden from the view of the goblins, they began to lay their mats on the ground to get some rest before returning to their den. Uka turned her back as Ilissa began to question herself and her previous experience: Where had the warmth gone? What happened to the light? Had she imagined the whole thing? She held back her whimpering as she gradually fell asleep.

Ilissa's dreams had always been more vivid than the rest of her cave family's dreams. She saw colors and pictures more clearly in her mind than she could with her eyes. She was surprised to find herself where her vision had left off: in the arms of a huge goblin. She saw familiar faces around her but felt real fear as she struggled in the goblin's grasp. A woman's scream caused her to turn in time to see a goblin's sword being pulled out of a man as he fell limp to the floor. Ilissa could feel herself shaking as she sobbed real tears, and darkness entered her open eyes.

She was back with Uka on the floor of the cave and surrounded by cold, dark stillness. Her eyes received no stimulus, but her ears heard a faint rumble beneath her. She peered down at the sleeping goblin guards and wondered if she was hearing them snore, but the noise she heard wasn't coming from them; it was coming from the other side of the wall of rubble. She saw no movement but heard sounds of rocks lightly grinding against each other, as if they were being moved. The last thing she saw was a blinding flash of light as a great explosion buried the goblins and knocked her unconscious.

"Run!" Brother Jason yelled to his three disciples from the mouth of the cave. "We will be praying for you."

Christopher took the lead as he tried his best to remember the path back to the troglodyte camp. The glow from their garments that seemed faint in the night sky seemed to intensify as they traveled deeper into the darkness of the cave. They carried no weapons with them, only medical supplies and enough provisions for a couple of days, but they immediately ran into their first obstacle.

They could smell her before they even heard her scream in terror. Uka began launching rocks at them from the passage above as she cursed and screamed for help. They took cover below the ledge, where Aaron and Evelyn began choking on the offensive odor. The rocks continued to rain down until Chris began grunting an explanation to the frightened and frightful girl. They exchanged grunts and groans until Chris finally signaled them it was safe to come out.

"What did you say to her?" Evelyn asked, while she gagged and covered her nose.

Chris roughly began explaining, "I told her I was looking for my family and that I am a lost son from the Ruokuri tribe. She said her name is Uka and that she and her sister were hurt in the explosion."

Evelyn raced ahead as she complained, "Brother Jason said no one was supposed to be here. What have we done? What did we get ourselves into?"

Uka held her arm as she grimaced in pain while blocking Evelyn from reaching her injured sister on the ground. Frustrated at first by the interference, Evelyn decided to turn her attention to Uka's wounds instead.

"Let me look at your arm," she said as she lowered her hood to expose her head and slowly reached for her medical supplies.

Uka's expression suddenly changed as she stared at Evelyn's face, while the glow from her garment caused Evelyn to pause as it revealed the wretched creature before her.

"Now hold still," she said as she reached for the girl's arm. "This will sting."

Screams of pain echoed through the cave as Evelyn poured disinfectant over Uka's wound, causing her to run away.

"What are you doing, Eve?" Aaron whispered. "The goblin army probably heard that scream all the way to their camp."

Evelyn just shook her head and rolled her eyes as she replied sarcastically, "What? You don't think they heard the extremely loud explosion and are on their way already? Come on, guys, pick that smelly girl off the ground and let's follow Uka before she gets away."

Nabal rushed through the dark corridors while barking commands to his small army, which followed closely behind him. Arriving at the site of the explosion and closely examining the debris, he quickly divided his troops, saying, "Muddle, Raff, you two go aboveground and find out who is responsible for this. You twenty, start blocking the passage with these boulders and stand guard. Just leave enough of an opening for my spies to fit through when they return. The rest of you, follow me."

Unaware of the shortcut through the narrow passage that led to the underground river, Nabal led his troops back the way they had come. Torches lit and swords in hand, they diverted to an alternative corridor that would eventually take them down to the troglodyte camp.

One of the twenty goblin soldiers who were left for cleanup duty began complaining, "Why do I always miss out on all the fun?" while the others began their tedious work of stacking the large boulders.

Another soldier found the remains of a Nephilim guard who was buried by the explosion. He motioned to the group while cackling and said, "Look! This one looks like my nutbutter and maggot sandwich after I digested it."

A roar of merriment filled the corridors as many of them rolled on the ground in laughter.

UNAMUSED BY THEIR DISCOVERY OR THEIR BANTER, a young goblin named Gog decided to begin an investigation of his own. His attempts to quiet the troops were met with ridicule, so he walked away and closed his eyes to focus on the other sounds of the cave.

His companions' hilarity dissipated as he moved farther away from them and placed his ear on the cave floor. He needed to consciously filter out the loudest noises so he could notice even the faintest sounds. Laughter gave way to rumbling and scraping rocks, which disappeared to uncover marching feet moving away from him. He questioned himself as he heard what appeared to be running water. Running water? The underground river was far from the mouth of the cave, wasn't it? As he focused harder, he finally heard what he was waiting for: a high-pitched voice that could only belong to a human girl.

Gog looked up and used the debris to climb to the exposed ledge. There was a strange scent that grew stronger with every step. He found more evidence of human activity as he reached the ledge to find a trail of blood, which led into a narrow passage. He felt his dark heart racing faster as the scent of not one but many humans grew stronger. He could feel the air turning cooler as he went farther into the opening. In his desperation to catch up with his prey, he slipped out of the path and into the moving currents of the underground river. Stunned by the cold and frantic to try to keep his head above water, he flailed like an injured animal as he was carried under and away by the slow-moving waters.

"Uka!" Evelyn yelled as they struggled to see, much less keep up with, her in the darkness.

"Maybe we should ask for Abba's help," Christopher said, panting as they stopped a while to rest.

"You do that," Aaron replied while he lay Ilissa on the ground. "I'll start looking for a good place to hide while we try to revive this girl. It'll be easier to have her guide us instead of us walking around lost in the dar …"

His reply was cut short by the brightening cavern. Christopher had knelt to pray, and his armor shone brighter than ever. Aaron couldn't help smiling at Evelyn as they simultaneously realized they were seeking the assistance of an unconscious girl instead of the help of an all-powerful God.

"There!" Evelyn said, pointing to a secluded opening by the cave wall.

They carefully carried Ilissa over the rough terrain as Christopher continued to pray. Once settled in this hideout, Evelyn began to treat Ilissa's wounds as Aaron prayed for her complete healing. They began to feel compassion for the girl, completely unaware that Abba had already led them to their lost sister.

After a few moments, Chris joined the group as they settled in for a well-deserved rest. "Is she going to be okay?" he asked as he put his bag under his head.

"We've done all we can for her," Aaron said. "The rest is up to Abba."

Evelyn yawned as she turned away from their bright armor and asked, "Won't the light from your armor lead them right to us?"

Christopher smiled as he replied, "If you're talking about the troglodytes, then the answer is no, because the light hurts their eyes. If you're talking about the goblins, the answer is still no, because Abba's light is invisible to their eyes. Just make sure you completely cover your entire body, including your head."

Satisfied with that statement, the three of them remained motionless as they joined Ilissa in the land of dreams.

CHAPTER TWELVE

Ilissa found herself standing among a large crowd in the middle of the large chamber where her people just celebrated Doo-rah, only this time, they were not reveling; instead, they were filled of fear. Terrified of the bright flames that surrounded them and the goblins that carried them, Ilissa just froze with a sense of helplessness as men, women, and children were being slaughtered before her eyes. She fell to her knees as a large muscular goblin singled her out and came straight for her.

Her wild, panic-stricken scream woke not only her, but also the young men who were next to her. Aaron tried his best to calm her as Christopher translated, trying to explain their situation. Ilissa struggled to see anything due to the brightness of their robes. She assumed that her dream was real and that her reality was just a dream.

⟹

"What's going on?" Evelyn asked as she stumbled into the hideout.

"Obviously, the girl is awake and afraid, Eve. Where were you?" Aaron asked, still trying to wake completely.

"I couldn't sleep, so I went for a walk. I don't have to explain myself to you," she answered, noticeably shaken.

Aaron examined her closely and remarked, "You look terrible."

"So do you, Aaron," she countered. "We all look and smell terrible. We are stuck in a terrible place and in a terrible situation. I don't know why I came down here with you guys. We are risking our lives hoping and wishing for a miracle. We're never going to save anyone, much less find Ilissa."

"Ilissa?" the young girl repeated clumsily.

"You know Ilissa?" Aaron asked the girl; he encouraged Chris to translate, and the two spoke for a minute.

He began, "She says that she heard someone whisper that name as he guided her to the wall of light rocks. She felt no fear and thought the voice was guiding her to the world above. She doesn't feel like she belongs here anymore."

Aaron didn't hear anything after Christopher said "whisper that name." He examined the girl's face as she and Chris continued to talk. She looked a little like a younger version of his mother and seemed to be around eleven years old: the age his baby sister would be now.

He prayed silently as he summoned the courage to ask her directly, "Are you Ilissa?"

She just smiled and repeated her name as she gradually opened her eyes wider.

"It's her! We found ... I mean, Abba has led us to her," Aaron exclaimed as he wrapped his arms around her.

Ilissa didn't understand why this man was holding her, and she instinctively bit his shoulder, causing him to retreat in surprise.

Chris laughed out loud at the sight of Aaron's reaction, while Evelyn seemed confused and pale, as if she had seen a spirit. "It can't be. What are the chances …" her voice trailed off as she slowly approached her younger sister. "What have they done to you?" she asked, holding her nose closed.

Composing himself, Aaron retrieved his gear and said, "We should get out here before we're discovered."

"What do you mean, Aaron?" asked Christopher.

"He means we've found Ilissa, and our mission is over," Evelyn snapped.

Christopher replied, "I can't believe how selfish you are. Our mission is far from over. Ilissa isn't the only person we need to save. There are hundreds, maybe thousands, of people down here who've never even heard the name of Abba, much less understood that there's a life of freedom on the surface. Are we just going to let them die without hearing the good news of the Emancipator?"

Aaron wondered if the darkness was affecting their hearts. Christopher turned to Ilissa, whose eyes were wide with apparent anxiety, and apologized on their behalf. He then asked, "Will you guide us to your family?"

Without knowing her true identity, and guided by the Spirit of Abba, she proclaimed in her own tongue that she would take them to her people, but her new place was among them.

MUDDLE AND RAFF HAD REACHED THE OUTSKIRTS OF Woodland by dawn. They wanted to do their best to impress their commander, but more than that, they wanted to outdo each other to impress their king. They had lost the scent of their prey and were competing with each other to see who would report the disappointing news to Nabal.

"It's your fault we lost their trail, so you should tell him," squealed Raff.

"I am your superior and am commanding you to file the report," Muddle barked back.

"Entering in the army before me doesn't make you my superior," countered Raff, as he lunged at his opponent.

"Maybe not," continued Muddle, "but my superior strength will force you to submit."

While wrestling on the ground, they inadvertently crashed through a concealed wooden door that led down some narrow stairs. Lying on the floor with the wind knocked out of them, they shook hands to form an uneasy truce and got up steadily. Their dark eyes adjusted quickly to the secret basement, which held a great variety of armor and weapons.

Looking thirstily at the barrels he thought contained wine, Raff said, "You know what I'm thinking?"

Without hesitating, Muddle walked past him and replied, "You're thinking these barrels are made from the same wood we found splintered throughout the mouth of the cave, and are probably filled with a highly flammable black powder which caused the explosion we were asked to investigate."

With that one statement, Muddle confirmed his superiority to Raff, as he could only reply, "Yeah! That's exactly what I was thinking."

Ilissa and her three companions from the world above traveled quickly through the labyrinth of walls and corridors that led back to her camp. As they drew closer, a feeling of dread seemed to suffocate her enthusiasm. Something was wrong, but she couldn't identify the source of her worries. She stopped to listen to the walls, and the other three followed her lead.

She abruptly sprinted over the path which led to the village, leaving the others far behind. The moans and cries of multitudes grew louder as the smell of blood grew stronger. She stopped at the edge of their encampment as a sea of lifeless bodies lay on a liquid red carpet.

"Ruok!" she cried out as her nightmare unfolded before her. "Uka, Aur, Ruok," she repeated, not caring who heard her.

A faint reply finally came and led her to her mortally wounded stepmother. Suffering from loss of blood and almost too weak to speak, the glow from her friends' robes caught the last word escaping from her lips: "Na-bal."

Carnage surrounded them as her visitors from above did their best to find and treat the injured masses in the darkness of the cavern. Ilissa dragged her stepmother's body to their shelter as she repeatedly screamed, "Uka, Aur, Uka, Aur!"

Her mind was a gallimaufry of anger, sadness, and fear as she desperately tried to compose herself. Had she gained three friends only to lose three family members? Why had she been called out and spared death? She searched internally for answers as she bathed her stepmother in her tears.

Ilissa didn't realize she had her eyes open until she saw a small, faint light floating toward her. She assumed it was one of the flying cave insects until she wiped away the droplets in her eyes that had blurred the image. The first indication that this was not a bioluminescent insect was its purple hue. The troglodytes had no word for "purple," since the only colors they had ever seen were the blue insects and the red goblin flames; this unfamiliar color seemed to be a mixture of both. Secondly, this glowing manifestation seemed to remove the darkness around her soul as it spoke her name and beckoned her to follow.

The only light outside her den were the robes of her three companions and the purple fire that slowly hovered about an arm's length away. She wasn't in a trance, but she did feel the anger and fear subside with every step she took. Before it disappeared, the purple light led her into a hidden crevice where her stepsisters, Uka and Aur, crouched, frozen in fear. Ilissa joined them in their grief as they hugged and huddled together until sleep overtook them.

BACK AT THE MAIN TROGLODYTE CAMP, THE THREE OUTSIDERS exhausted their medical supplies, their energy, and their hope as they moved from person to person. They tried in vain to communicate with the survivors who, for the most part, hid in the darkness from the strangers with the armor of light. Some of the wounded hissed and scratched at them as they covered their eyes from the blinding glow.

"Can't they see we're trying to help them, Chris?" an exasperated Aaron asked, as he received a bite from a crippled boy.

"They are offended by our smell and the light from our robes," Christopher explained.

"We offend them?" Evelyn asked sarcastically. "They are the ones who reek of death and disease. My head and stomach ache, and I'm tired. Let's just get Ilissa and go."

Aaron stood in agreement, suddenly realizing it had been hours since they had last seen their sister.

"Where is she?" he asked, in a state of panic. "This can't be happening. Is it possible that we've lost her again?"

His unnerving echoes reverberated off the walls and through the corridors while sending the cave dwellers fleeing to their hiding spots.

"Be quiet, Aaron!" Evelyn commanded, as she grabbed his robe with one fist and covered his mouth with the other hand. "Whoever did this could come back at any moment and finish the job. I didn't come here to die, brother. Now calm down and help me find Ilissa."

Aaron's concern for one sister suddenly turned to concern for the other, as he gazed into Evelyn's empty eyes. Her face seemed drained of all color, and her breath smelled like fermented fruit. He wondered if he looked as bad she did, as he examined his dirty hands and both of their stained robes. He glanced at the tooth marks on his arm and then at the crippled boy who had given them to him, dragging himself away from them. He saw the panic in the boy's eyes as he looked over his shoulder one last time before disappearing into the shadows.

"Abba," Aaron whispered as he fell to his knees, "forgive me for focusing on myself and my fears instead of the mission. We aren't here for pleasure or revenge. All these people need to know your love, and my frustration is getting in the way. Please keep us safe from the enemy and give us the strength to complete this great commission you have entrusted us. Help us find Ilissa and our way out with as many people as possible. In Iam's name, I beg you. Amen."

"Someone's coming," Chris said, as the light from Aaron's robe illuminated the great hall.

The three figures walked slowly toward them as they shielded their eyes from the intense brightness.

"It's Ilissa and two other girls!" Evelyn said, as she ran to meet them.

Chris and Aaron thanked Abba for such a quick reply as they began making plans to return home.

CHAPTER THIRTEEN

The orphanage had been a safe haven for the people of Woodland since it was built and throughout the goblin wars. Many of the rooms remained a secret to both humans and goblins. Not even the Goblin King himself knew about the sub-basement armory or about its hidden entrance in the forest. Muddle and Raff thought about the reward they would receive from Nabal and the promotion they would get from their king, as they piled the assortment of weapons on the forest floor.

"Muddle," Raff said, wheezing for every breath, "wouldn't it be faster if I went back to the cave for some help from the rest of our crew? This is taking all day."

Muddle looked at him sternly as he replied, "Do you think I'm so dense that I'll let you take full credit for our discovery? Just stick to the plan, and let me worry about the details. Once we finish getting all the useful items out of the room, we can dip this rope in tar, place it in an open barrel filled with the black powder, and light it on fire. There are enough explosives down there to make the whole building collapse. We'll do more damage in one day than the entire goblin army did in ten years. Do you really want to share the glory with our brothers?"

Raff's smile said more than a thousand words as he ignored his weariness and continued his monotonous trek down the dark stairs.

FURTHER DOWN THAN ANY FLIGHT OF STAIRS COULD DE- scend or any ray of starlight could reach, the three glowing messengers uncovered their heads to proclaim the reason for their arrival to anyone who would hear. The troglodytes gathered to hear the story of Iam as recorded in the Histories, as Chris began expounding the good news to them in their own tongue and for the first time in their lives.

They heard about Ish's deception, which led human- ity into captivity, and Abba's plan to rescue them. They listened intently as he spoke about how their Creator became a perfect, sinless man Who lived among them for thirty-three years until he gave his life to make a way out of the darkness.

"We know the way to a new life," Christopher said in their dialect. "Follow us to freedom. Follow Iam and become a new creation. He is the way."

The sound that followed Chris's invitation was a se- ries of groans that everyone understood to mean "blas- phemy." The crowd parted to make way for the high priest, who seemed to glide across the floor, with his staff pointed his directly at Chris. His gray hair matched his skin and eyes, and if not for his piercings and cere- monial tattoos, they would've mistaken him for a spirit.

As the priest spoke fear into the people, Aaron received a revelation from Abba. Through a vision, he saw the same dragon's hand that tried to grab baby Ilissa, controlling the high priest like a puppet. Then the priest's head fell awkwardly to his shoulder, as his empty and snakelike eyes pointed directly toward Aaron. The feeling of crawling insects on his entire body made it obvious to him that the priest was possessed by their greatest enemy.

"We come in Abba's name, and you have no power over us," Aaron said with authority, as he raised his hand toward the man.

The priest smiled a wicked smile as his lifeless body fell to the ground, but the priest's deceptive words had already taken effect. Most of the troglodytes scurried back into the darkness as the sounds of a marching army came within earshot.

"He was just a distraction to get us to expose ourselves," Evelyn moaned.

"There are the children of light," Maruffo said as he guided Nabal and his army into the grand hall.

The goblin army rushed like ants from every corridor as they surrounded Chris, Aaron, Evelyn, Ilissa, and her two stepsisters. With their heads uncovered, the three surface dwellers were just as visible as the three cave dwellers. Nabal barked his command to freeze while he made his way to the group of captives. Maruffo walked ahead of the pack, like a predator surveying his prey, as he smiled and said, "What right do you have to trespass in to the king's domain and steal his property? Are you here to start another war with us, children?"

"We are not children, nor are we your property," Chris snapped defiantly. "We are Abba's ambassadors, and we know our legal rights."

Nabal chuckled as he countered, "Is that right? Well, then, if we can't enslave you, then I suppose we'll have to kill you."

He raised his huge, dull blade just as Ilissa screamed, "Abba!" at the top of her lungs. At the same moment, there was a rumbling, and the earth began to shake around them. Stalactites came crashing down around the young group, crushing every goblin they could see but leaving them completely untouched.

The humans were the only ones who remained standing as they turned to look at Ilissa.

"What just happened?" Aaron asked, dumfounded.

Ilissa had no special powers, and she looked as surprised as any of them as they searched their own minds for an explanation.

Chris blurted, "There must've been a huge explosion aboveground. We must hurry home and see if our brothers and sisters are all right."

The moving earth beneath them confirmed that it was time to flee, as the immortal goblins began to groan and free themselves from the debris that buried them. Aaron and Chris led the way, while Evelyn tried to calm the three younger girls as goblin hands began to shoot out from the ground, trying to keep them from leaving. The young men's robes began to brighten as they dusted themselves off and asked Abba for guidance and protection so they could all get home safely.

While passing the dark fields, their focus on escaping was interrupted by growls and screams coming from behind them. Aaron's heart sank as he turned to see nothing but shadows of bodies grappling and wrestling on the floor. His sunken heart broke as his robe's light revealed his disheveled sister with black liquid oozing from her mouth and a half-eaten passion fruit in her hands.

"Evelyn, what are you doing?" Aaron asked in complete shock as Ilissa and her stepsisters cried helplessly behind her.

"I was just trying to pick some fruit to take with us, when these simpletons attacked me for no reason."

The scratches on the girls confirmed their struggle; Chris rushed over to console them. Evelyn's expressionless face reminded him of that first night she went missing in the cave. The fermented breath he had smelled on her previously had confirmed what he was too busy, or too unwilling, to accept. She had tasted the forbidden fruit and was now addicted to it.

"Put the fruit down, Eve. We need to go now," Aaron cried as he reached for the fruit she held tightly in her hands.

She answered him with a hiss, exposing her blackened teeth to him and snarling, "Only if I can bring the fruit with me."

Chris cautiously guided the girls around Aaron and Evelyn as he accepted her decision, even though it was against Abba's desire for her.

The light inside Aaron battled Evelyn's darkness, as he tried to persuade her to let go of the temporal pleasure she had in her hands and instead choose eternal joy in Abba's promises.

"How could you return to the cave once you've tasted freedom, Evelyn?" Aaron asked desperately.

Evelyn took another bite of the fruit as she answered dopily, "I never chose to come out of the cave. I was an infant when Freddie carried me out, remember? No, I guess you don't remember, since we've been lied to most of our lives. How can we trust the Brotherhood if we couldn't even trust our parents? How do we know the Histories are true? How do we even know Abba's real?"

"You've seen His creation," replied Aaron, "and His power, and His deliverance. He's given us many great victories over our enemies, and He led us to Ilissa. How could you deny His existence?"

Chris tugged at his arm, trying to get him to accept her choice. Evelyn just smiled eerily as she gazed into nothingness and continued to indulge herself with another fruit.

Chris forcefully pulled Aaron away from her as he tried to console him, saying, "Even though Iam has made a way of escape for everyone, He knows many will choose the darkness and their own passions instead. Everyone who comes to Him must do so willingly."

At that moment, Aaron recalled a dream he had had at the orphanage the night before his father's funeral. Inexplicitly, he felt heat as he saw light coming from a cavern in front of him. Once again, he saw his baby sister crying on the floor, as he knelt just a few feet away. As he crawled closer, his infant sister turned to him, revealing her face for the first time. It wasn't Ilissa, as he had previously assumed. It was baby Evelyn.

"I told you she was mine," a voice in his head boasted, as they all heard a thundering chuckle echoing throughout the cavern.

The Goblin King's laugh was joined by Evelyn as she fell deeper into his influence.

"No!" Aaron screamed. "As long as there is breath in my lungs, strength in my body, and a glimmer of hope … I will try to save my sister."

He pushed Christopher aside as he made up his mind to fight the entire goblin army single-handedly, if necessary.

A shriek from behind him caused him to stop and turn around as he saw a lone goblin scout holding a sharpened stalactite to his little sister's neck.

"You can take the girl out of the cave, but you can't take the cave out of the girl," Gog said as he brandished his prisoner with pride. "Even if you escaped with her, what makes you think she won't come back to the underworld?"

Aaron knew that the goblin was talking about Ilissa, but the words rang true about Evelyn, as well. Would he focus on the sister who wanted to stay or save the one who wanted to escape?

"Your choice is simple," Gog said, sneering. "You surrender to me, or I kill the girls, one by one."

Aaron's swift decision was clear but not easy. He covered his head, making himself disappear, while Chris closed his eyes and said to the confused goblin, "Our battle isn't against flesh and blood. You've already lost and don't even know it."

His robe shone brighter than ever as he asked Abba to deliver them from evil, which caused the goblin to drop his weapon as he covered his eyes in pain. Aaron picked up the sharpened rock and knocked him out with the dull end before he even had a chance to defend himself.

Christopher hesitated as he walked over the unconscious goblin; he looked toward his friend and asked, "Are you ready to go now?"

Aaron sighed heavily and said, "Only if you promise to come back with me to save my sister."

Chris paused and then agreed, "I will come back with you so we can rescue as many people as we can."

The marching army behind them kept them moving quickly through the tunnels as they crossed the underground river to the cliff that overlooked their escape route. Only one obstacle remained.

"There's about twenty goblins down there," Chris said. "How are only two robes supposed to conceal five of us?"

Aaron reminded Chris of Brother Jason's plan to create a distraction, but he was concerned about the timing. Ilissa, Uka, and Aur didn't understand what the young men were saying, but they could clearly see the anxiety in the young men's faces.

Just then, Aur, the youngest member of the group, fell to her knees and began communicating with her unseen Creator. One by one, her sisters joined her on the ground, as they seemed to pray for a miracle. Peace overcame Aaron's fear as he and Chris joined the girls on their knees.

Since the goblin guards had finished their job of blocking most of the opening, and there was no sign of Muddle or Ruff returning, they became bored. While most of them slept, one alert goblin sniffed the air as he woke the others to ask, "Do you smell that?"

Aaron stopped praying and felt his heart would stop as well, while Chris and the girls just kept pleading for Abba's salvation. All the goblins rose with their noses testing the air, and as soon as they spoke the word, it came ... "Water!"

A flood of rushing water went as fast as it came through the lower portion of the cave entrance, taking with it almost all signs of their enemies. Aur squealed with joy as she rushed down to the narrow opening, holding her sisters with each hand. Aaron and Chris stood awestruck as they saw the swift and powerful answer to their prayer clear the way for their escape.

The girls ran down quickly and began to go through the opening chronologically. First Aur, then Ilissa, but Uka hesitated as her smile slowly disappeared and blood began to stain her garment. A silent arrow had hit its mark as a band of immortal goblins had recovered from the partial cave collapse and caught up to the escaping children. Maruffo cackled hysterically from the ledge they had stood on only seconds ago, while flaming arrows rained down. Aaron commanded Chris to take the younger girls ahead while he carried Uka out himself.

The goblin horde raced behind them like a pack of wild animals, seeking to satisfy their thirst for vengeance. They were stopped cold by a huge boulder rolling down from the mouth of the cave; it crushed the pursuing goblins and put a stop to their pursuit. The rescue was complete, and they were safe for now.

Aaron mournfully carried Uka's body into the forest as they looked for a place to bury her. They arrived at a clearing and used branches to dig a shallow grave, as her stepsisters lamented over another loss to their family. The cool night air and star-speckled sky provided a perfect backdrop as Chris spoke words of comfort to the grieving sisters. He explained that the end of this life means the beginning of another one.

"To be apart from our bodies here is to be present with Abba in eternity," he began. "You have been called out of the cave for a reason, just as I was many years ago. And even if we are young and have suffered much, the peace we have knowing that Abba is gathering all his children into his presence brings us comfort. Morning will rise like a curtain, signifying the beginning of another act to our story."

Fading darkness turned into glorious light.

EPILOGUE

Far away, in a place of perpetual light, where neither time nor space have any effect, a lone beautiful creature marched toward his Master. His muscular, radiant body grew more peaceful with every step. Michael, commander of the heavenly army, humbly walked past his troops, knowing there was no fear or envy in their eyes as he ambled to his destination. He would never get tired of the beautiful sights around him that seemed to caress his face with every step and fill his soul with love.

He felt the time had come for his report, and even though his Master was omniscient, he was the one who needed the assurance that everything was going as planned. He loved his responsibilities, his brothers, his perfect environment, but most of all, he loved his Master. In the failed coup that led one-third of his brothers into a nightmarish abyss, he knew he had made the right choice in following the Creator. The only thing that brought Michael more joy than his present condition was the hope of a brighter future.

The increase of tranquility, and the radiant light piercing two large pearl gates, meant he had arrived at his destination. He smiled at his fellow brothers, who quickly opened the gates for him to enter the King's chamber. After taking only a few steps, the Glory overtook him, and he fell to his knees in worship. On the throne sat Iam, immersed in unapproachable light, surrounded by a host of heavenly beings who sang, "Holy, Holy, Holy is our loving Abba. Who was, and is, and is to come."

Michael, unable to rise or look up, joined in the chorus, and then Iam stood to his feet and spoke. Visible waves could be seen pulsating with every word that came from the Father of Lights.

"Michael, my son, what can I do for you?" the King inquired of his commander.

"Abba, forgive my restlessness, but I know you are aware of the children's escape from the cave. You promised you would return for them at the end of time to bring justice to their enemies who persecute them relentlessly. Has that time come, my Lord?"

As Iam walked toward him, the glorious light of Abba remained on the throne. He radiated with light and love as He offered His calloused hands to His friend and helped him rise to his feet.

Michael felt a sadness in Iam as he looked directly into his moist eyes; He replied, "My children have suffered much, but their present troubles won't last very long. Yet they produce a glory that vastly outweighs them and will last forever." Iam held Michael's strong, chiseled face in his battered hands and continued, "I'm not being slow about my promise, as you may think. No, I am being patient for their sake. I do not want anyone to be destroyed, but I want everyone to repent."

Iam then hugged Michael as he whispered into his ear, "Only three more of My children remain in the cave, and as soon as they hear My voice and realize their true identity, I will return to execute judgment on the wicked. So you, too, must keep watch. For you do not know the day or hour of my return."

An indescribable peace entered Michael as he cast his cares on his Master and said, "Amen. May Your grace be upon Your people until then."

To be concluded …

LESSONS FROM
THE CAVE

The purpose of this devotional is to guide family conversations and expand on some of the biblical concepts from *The Cave*. It is intended to enhance your understanding of the book and, more importantly, bring you closer as a family. Adjust this devotional tool to meet your family's needs. Expect fidgeting, and pray for wisdom and patience as your family goes through each chapter. My prayer is that by the end of the journey, you will have grown closer to each other and to our Savior.

ONE

1. How would you describe Aaron and Evelyn's relationship, and how can they improve it?

2. Is it easy for you to make friends? Make a list of the qualities you look for in a friend and compare them to your character strengths.

3. Read Romans 15:1 and talk about how you can use your character strengths to help others with their weaknesses.

4. God loves you and uses people and situations around you to expose your weaknesses so you can discipline yourself. If you get angry at a person, or walk away from a difficult situation, you are walking away from God's discipline. Read Proverbs 3:11-12 and ask God in your own words to show you your weaknesses and how the people around you can help you grow a more Christlike character.

TWO

1. What would be the best part of adding a new member to your family?

2. What's the hardest thing about sharing your space and stuff?

3. Compare how the Freeman family treated their guest to the way the Goblin King treated his servant. Jesus teaches us to treat others the way we want to be treated. Talk about a time you didn't follow this Golden Rule and what you learned from the experience.

4. Memorize 1 Peter 4:9 and discuss how your family can use time, talents, and resources to help someone this week.

THREE

Note to parents: Although this story is fictional, this chapter may raise many real concerns in young readers. Remind them that God has given us guardians, police, and armed forces to protect us from visible threats in addition to prayer and his Holy Spirit to protect us from invisible forces. Use the following Bible verses to guide your children through their questions and pray that they find peace in God's promises:

> "[Nothing] is able to separate us from the love of God" (Romans 8:38–39).

> "I go to prepare a place for you" (John 14:1–6).

> "No more death" (Revelation 21:4).

God's promises are only for His children, but today you are being invited to be part of His family so you can claim these promises for yourself. The only thing that stands in your way is sin, but God has the power to forgive all your sin right now.

Would you like for God to wash away your sin and adopt you into His family?

It's as easy as ABC:

- Admit that you have sinned and ask Him to forgive you.
- Believe that His love and forgiveness is stronger than your sin.
- Confess Him as your King and Savior.

If you have decided to be part of God's family, write down today's date to remind you of your "spiritual birthday"

Name: Date:

_____   _____

_____   _____

_____   _____

_____   _____

Welcome to God's family! This is the beginning of your new life of loving God more than sin. Now you can claim the Bible's promises for yourself and pray that He uses you to guide others to Himself.

"Most assuredly, I say to you, he who hears My word and believes in Him who sent Me has everlasting life, and shall not come into judgment, but has passed from death into life" (John 5:24).

FOUR

Families come in all sizes, but they start with only two people: a man and a woman.

1. Although families vary in number, read Matthew 18:20 to see how God blesses even the smallest families who seek Him together.

In Genesis 2:24, the Bible introduces marriage as the foundation of the family. God intended the family to function like a small church to spread His message of salvation.

2. How do we work together to expand God's kingdom here on earth?

3. How can we set a better example to our neighbors so they can follow God?

Sometimes, bad things happen that alter the family structure, but many times, these changes are normal and even ordained by God (for example, children grow and start their own families). Families change because people change; no two families are exactly alike.

4. Whose family needs our prayer right now?

We don't have to be born to our parents to be loved by them. Many people add to their family through the process of adoption. An orphan being adopted is a clear example of what happens to us when we join God's family.

5. Read and discuss Psalm 10:14 and John 14:18–21, remembering to pray daily so God's children may return to Him as He promises to return for us.

FIVE

1. An emancipator is someone who sets people free. In this book he is called Iam. Does the book's description remind you of someone from the Bible?

2. The Hypostatic Union is the biblical teaching that Jesus was 100 percent God and 100 percent human while on earth (see John 1:1-3, 14 and Colossians 2:9). God's invisible, living Word was surrounded by a human body while still remaining divine. Does this doctrine make sense to you?

3. In John 15:13, what is defined as the "greatest love"?

4. How does it make you feel to know that our God humbled Himself and gave His life to set us free from the guilt and eternal punishment of our sin?

5. The goblins represent our spiritual enemies who have been stripped of their power by Jesus. The Bible is full of examples where He showed His authority over all of the fallen angels, including

their king. Read how Jesus, the living Word, used the spoken Word of God to defeat his greatest enemy in Matthew 4:1–11 (then ask Him to fight for you as well).

SIX

The loss of any loved one leaves us with a void that nobody can replace and only God can fill. The amount of time it takes to heal from emotional scars depends on many factors, but our dependence and faith in our heavenly Father will carry us through the most difficult seasons. Take a few moments to thank Him for your life and ask Him to use you to help hurting people every day.

1. The orphanage in the book represents our church buildings, which is where we are fed spiritually (and sometimes physically) and learn more about God's plan for the world. How can our home be more like a church?

2. People who don't believe in God sometimes try to change history in order to live their lives without Him, not realizing it is "His story." What are some of the things you've heard at school or seen on TV or the computer that make you question the way the Bible records history?

3. Explain Patricia's "stolen pet" story in your own words. Read Romans 5:18–19 and simplify this teaching by using the following example: The owner of the tree also owns the fruit.

Next time you hear someone say, "It's not fair that we all die because of Adam's sin," you can respond in love by saying, "It's not fair that Jesus died because of yours."

SEVEN

1. The goblin's passion fruit can be used to symbolize anything that you struggle with or something that becomes more important to you than God. What is something in your life that keeps you from getting closer to God? Could this "passion" turn into an obstacle to spread the gospel or an addiction to you?

2. In the story, Clara and Jason quoted John 10:10, which was first spoken by Jesus. Read this verse from your Bible and talk about the contrast between what the enemy offers and what God offers. How can we use our words and actions to produce the "abundant life" in our family and community?

3. After Aaron prayed for his baby sister, he felt a supernatural peace fill his soul, mind, and body. Read Philippians 4:6–7 and share with your family a time when you prayed for them and felt God's peace.

4. God tries to guide us through His Holy Spirit, but many times, we aren't paying attention or choose to ignore Him. God also places people in our lives at critical times to try to guide us. Aaron chose to listen to Jason instead of letting his rage control him. Who has God put in your life to help you make better decisions?

EIGHT

Did you know that you are a spirit surrounded by a human body? It's true. The person you see when you look in the mirror is just a protective shell for the real "you" inside. Don't misunderstand me; the material world you see and experience (trees, animals, people, etc.) is just as real as the invisible realm. The only difference is that all the material things are temporary, while the invisible things are eternal (2 Corinthians 4:18).

1. What do you think about the fact that you're going to exist forever?

2. Where do you think you're going to spend eternity and why?

The cave dwellers symbolize the people who are living in spiritual darkness. They are just like us in that they have jobs, go to school, have families, and take care of each other. The only difference is that they are slaves of sin because they don't follow Jesus.

3. Read Romans 6:23 together and talk about how we can help our friends and family to know and follow Jesus.

4. Have you noticed that some of the laws and rules of this world contradict what the Bible teaches as good?

5. Why do you think most people ignore God and the Bible's teachings?

NINE

1. Ten years have passed since Ilissa was taken into the cave. How have Aaron and Evelyn changed? How are they the same?

2. How is it possible that, for the most part, the cave dwellers were unaware of the war between the goblins and the surface dwellers? What do you think about your friends and family who are unaware of the spiritual war that has been going on since the beginning of time?

The cave dwellers were too distracted by their passions and celebrations to notice the war going on around them. In Isaiah 5:13, the prophet talks about how God's people went into slavery for their lack of knowledge about their purpose. In Mark 7:13, Jesus also mentions how we may place our traditions over God's Word. Is it possible that our opinions, our traditions, and even our festivities dilute the message of the gospel and keep the lost people enslaved?

This week, do some research on the origins of a holiday or celebration of your choice and share your findings with your family. After prayerful consideration, discuss how you can make your celebrations more Christ-focused so that your loved ones can hear, and hopefully receive, God's invitation to join His family.

TEN

It's important to remember to start off every day in prayer and ask God for His guidance and protection. In the story, the main characters were given the armor of light to protect them in the dark cave. We have also been given a spiritual armor by our heavenly Father to protect us in this spiritually dark world.

1. Read Ephesians 6:10–19 together and imagine prayerfully putting on each part of the armor of God.

2. Why is it important to protect your mind and your heart every day?

The world around us may seem good and normal until we immerse ourselves with God's teachings and spend time with godly people (1 John 2:15–17, Hebrew 10:25).

3. Have you noticed anything in yourself that is offensive to God? Can one of your family members

    lovingly help you work on a sinful area in your life?

4. In the story, Ilissa heard Abba whispering her name. In the Bible, Elijah also heard God calling him in a soft voice (1 Kings 19:11–13). What are some things that might prevent you from hearing from God?

God may not speak to you audibly, but he continues to speak to His children through His Holy Spirit and His written Word. Just like a physical sword, the sword of the Spirit takes practice to use correctly, so study it daily.

ELEVEN

1. Ilissa's adoptive family had a hard time understanding why she wanted to follow God's voice. What difficulties have you had with people misunderstanding your desire to follow Christ?

2. Not only did Ilissa's behavior change, but her desires did, as well. How are your passions lining up with God's will now that you're part of His family?

For those of us who've been in God's family for a long time, it might be hard to mingle with our unsaved friends and family. Their words and actions may seem offensive to us, but it is necessary that we get beyond our differences and speak to their heart (Romans 10:14–15). We find many passages in Scripture where Jesus helped the undesirable and offensive people of His time. Read Matthew 8:1–3 and discuss how He touched an unclean leper to heal him; how can we follow His example?

Even though we may love the lost people in this world and have the best intentions to share the gospel with them, it is ultimately up to the Holy Spirit to convince them to repent and surrender their lives to Jesus (John 16:8–9). Praying for them is our first and best option before sharing the good news.

TWELVE

Even though we are trying to save people from an eternity without God, many of them misinterpret our sharing the gospel with them as an act of hate instead of an act of love.

1. Read John 15:18–19 and encourage each other to continue sharing the gospel in spite of the negative reactions you've received.

2. Many Christians around the world today are being persecuted, attacked, and even killed for their devotion to God. Spend a few minutes praying for our brothers and sisters around the world.

Jesus's Great Commission to us is found in Matthew 28:19–20. Read and discuss how we may not be able to reach the entire world with the gospel, but how our offerings and prayers help our church family to spread the message of salvation worldwide.

THIRTEEN

In the book, Chris studied and used his knowledge of his people to proclaim the good news to them.

1. What gifts and talents can you use and develop to expand God's kingdom?

2. What gifts and talents are you willing to develop to be more effective in sharing the good news? Are you willing to learn a new language, develop a new skill, or even move to another part of the world?

The book of Daniel recounts the story of three young Hebrew men who chose to trust God, even in the face of certain death. Read their account starting in chapter 3 verses 11–30 and discuss their bold response to the king in verses 17–18:

3. Should we fear death and give in to ungodly laws (2 Corinthians 5:8)?

4. Will God always spare us from physical death?

5. Read Romans 8:32–34 and discuss the cost of freedom and the eternal reward for those who are citizens of heaven.

Even though God doesn't want anyone to die without knowing Him (2 Peter 3:9), He knows many will choose their own temporary passions over His eternal love and forgiveness. Even so, we must continue to pray for, and preach to, the lost, since only God knows the final outcome of their choices.

God has a plan to redeem His children; will you be a part of it?

Printed in the United States
By Bookmasters